Onion Man
The
Smelliest Hero

Also by Chad Retterath:

Notes on Monster Hunting

Weapons of Disharmony

Tales from Ruun

Cover art by Miguel González

Dedicated to my dad.
Thanks for teaching me
all about fart jokes.

Part I
The Malodorous
Onion Man

An Introduction

A city without a hero is like a farm without a farmer. Things grow wherever they please and the insects and animals that suffer from an insatiable hunger ravage the landscape. And the farm is even worse. Delicalopolis is not that type of disgusting, wild city. It has a hero, who happens to be the smelliest of all heroes.

A weak breeze blew through his ravishing golden hair, and the sun danced delightfully in his courageous eyes. He was a handsome hero. A hero of looks with impressive abs, a chiseled jaw, and armpits full of foul, horrific smells.

He posed heroically on top of the tallest building in Delicalopolis. It was a 413 floor tall arcade with eighteen floors dedicated to pinball. Onion Man wobbled, almost losing his balance. He took a deep breath in, puffed out his chest, and pretended he was ready to stop all of the corruption in his beloved city.

Sirens wailed in the distance, echoing through the streets. With his marvelous eyesight, Onion Man saw an intense police chase five blocks away. His heroic instincts, which every hero should have, told him that his assistance was desperately needed below. With the grace of a newborn piglet, he jumped from the skyscraper. The wind rushed past as he maneuvered himself into a flying position. He stretched out his left arm and put his legs straight out with his feet pointed. During his fall, Onion Man remembered that he forgot how to fly. The highway charged towards him, and with a mighty splat, he collided with the pavement. Dust and debris shot in every direction.

Through the dust came the criminal leading the police in a chase of speed and wits in his brand new, most likely stolen, sports car. Onion Man tried to push himself up off of the cold road. Before he stood the criminal hit him as if he wasn't a superhero, but a giant speed bump. The axles ripped off the car, causing it to slide fifty feet down the highway before coming to a screeching halt.

Onion Man stood up, smoothed out his suit, and brushed the dust off his masculine chest. A police officer strutted up to the hero, who smiled at her. He felt like he had accomplished a heroic deed, but the officer glared at him with a look that pierced through his masculinity.

"What in the world were you trying to do? You destroyed this highway," shouted the officer.

"I was only trying to help," said Onion Man. His ears hurt. They were far too close for shouting to be necessary.

"Well don't try to help again. You never do. You just make things worse. Just give up. You're more useless than an onion," yelled the officer.

Onion Man's eyes filled with tears. He felt as if he had just lost his onions as well as his pride. A gust of wind knocked the officer over as he began running away at full speed, loudly crying like a baby.

During the tear-filled sprint back to his lair, he heard a call for help. He stopped running and used his superhero hearing to detect the silent alarm from a nearby store. After his embarrassment moments ago, he knew assisting would be a horrible idea, but the call was irresistible. The call for justice needed to be answered.

Onion Man heroically pranced into the local dollar store. Inside, three men had the cashier at gunpoint. Two of the men gently held the same handgun as a team, while the man who looked like the leader because of his elegant tie, held his own freshly polished firearm. The leader pointed his gun at Onion Man and said, "Don't come any further or I will shoot. Don't try to be a hero."

Onion Man bolted like a bulldozer at the criminal. Immediately, the criminal shot the gun, but the bullet bounced off Onion Man's powerful pectoral muscles. The hero kept charging forward in a maniacal stampede. When they crashed into the cement wall, Onion Man caught a glimpse of the explosives attached to the criminal's chest. The collision triggered the explosives, detonating them in a fiery eruption. The dollar store collapsed in a puff and poof with flair and dust. Moments later, police officers and the mayor arrived at the scene.

The mayor, a fat pear-shaped man with frizzy orange hair, walked up to the edge of the destroyed building. "Onion Man... we need to have a talk. Come to City Hall with me, okay?" Onion Man nodded and stepped out of the ruins. He reluctantly leaned down and fell into the mayor's limo. Onion Man laid face down on the seat with his legs bent against the door. The mayor's expression was filled with pure embarrassment while he looked down at the failed hero. "Onion Man..." the mayor cut himself off when Onion Man looked up with false hope leaking out of his eyes. "Never mind. Please, put your head back down." Snot and tears pushed their way through the hero's ridiculously manly face. He slammed his face into the seat, causing the whole limo to shake and swerve.

The limo reached the street leading to City Hall. News reporters and Delicalopians filled the area. The mayor stepped out of the limo once it stopped in front of the building. Onion Man dragged himself out of the limo and flopped onto the cement. He rolled forward onto his feet and followed the mayor up the enormous staircase. Step after step a little onion gas squeaked from the hero, but he assumed nobody would notice. At the top of the stairs, a podium with a large microphone waited for the two men. The mayor happily stepped onto the small stool behind the podium and adjusted the microphone to his height. He took a breath in to begin, but the crowd at the bottom of the stairs started to retreat in horror. Reporters started to vomit and faint from what they later reported as 'a strong, horribly onion-scented smell,' which is also known as a heroic fart from a heroic man.

The mayor looked at the hero standing beside him. Onion Man had his legs spread wide with his hands on his hips. It was what he called his 'heroic pose'. The mayor rolled his eyes before looking back and giving the city a fake smile.

"Today we have brought Onion Man to the center of the city that he's destroying, our precious Delicalopolis. In a single day, this hero nearly destroyed our most valuable highway, the one named after me, and our most profitable dollar store, the one I own," said the mayor.

Onion Man's big manly jaw started to twitch. He used all of his heroic will to hold back the tears.

"And that's only today," continued the mayor. "Onion Man has been our city's hero for years and has never done anything useful or cool." He looked over to Onion Man. "Other heroes do cool things. Why don't you?"

"Well," said Onion Man loudly. "I want to—"

A giant ball of ice struck the building behind Onion Man and the mayor. The collision sent cracks slithering out in the cement. The whole building shuttered and creaked. Onion Man and the mayor turned and watched as the City Hall collapsed. The crowd muttered and made bird noises while they acted surprised. They tried to act like crowds normally do during scary events in movies. Somebody screamed and ran away, but she stopped once she crossed the street and began walking normally.

People in the crowd started to fly out to the side as a figure skated past them. He punched or pushed every citizen he passed, even if they weren't in his way. The man stood about four and a half feet tall with ice crystals for hair and had an iron mask covering his face. He stopped and stood, much more heroically than Onion Man, at the bottom of the stairs.

"Look," yelled a voice in the crowd, "it's Solid Water Guy."

"What? Who said that?" The man turned and looked for the voice. He cleared his throat. "I'm Ice Man. This is now my city," announced Ice Man.

The mayor shrugged. "Alright. I hope you enjoy it." He stepped away from the podium and started to walk into the sagging building.

Onion Man looked at the mayor, completely appalled that he surrendered so easily. He turned back and lunged at the villain. Ice Man stepped out of the way, but Onion Man's momentum brought him straight down the stairs, then through the cement. His legs and backside stuck into the air while his head and torso were three feet into the ground. Ice Man shot an ice ball at Onion Man's gas shooter, freezing the hero in a block of ice. The villain dashed at Onion Man and kicked, causing the ice to shatter. Onion Man was launched out of the ground and over the crowd. He crashed down into the street, forming a little crater. The hero stood up to see a bus driving straight at him.

"Awesome," said Onion Man. The bus struck him, throwing his head back into the road. He laid in his Onion Man shaped crater for a couple of minutes before standing up. He felt flustered and decided to head back to his lair. He climbed the numerous staircases until he got to his second-level apartment in the northwest side of Delicalopolis. Potato chips cracked as he stepped into his filthy living space. Or lair. Apartment lair. Onion Man sat down in a recliner made out of sadness and mold. With his amazing intellect, the hero pushed a button on the remote next to him to turn on his five-inch high-definition television.

The amazingly beautiful, awful, ugly evening news anchor for Channel Fourteen Delicate News was on at City Hall. She stood holding her microphone with her back to the building. Ice Man could be seen strutting around freezing women, children, and small puppies. The horror.

"Today our local 'superhero' has been defeated in an embarrassing fight against the new supervillain, and amazingly handsome, Ice Man. Shortly after the fight, Onion Man disappeared from the City Hall and he has not been seen since. It is assumed he is somewhere else," said the news anchor.

Onion Man started to cry like the manly man he always pretends to be. "I'm done helping this city. They don't appreciate me. I'm taking a vacation," said Onion Man to himself.

Stomping came from the floor above him. "Shut up. I'm trying to watch the news," yelled the man upstairs.

Onion Man took off running as fast as he could, which was really fast. He crossed the great ocean and the not as great sea. After days of constant running, he arrived at his home, Onion Island. It was time for what every superhero needs, months of chronic training, and a bath.

Onion Island, a pile of sand with an enormous palm tree that produced coconut shaped onions, sat right in the middle of the Atlantic Ocean. Onion Man took off his filthy spandex suit and hung it on an Onion Tree branch. Yellow, brown, orange, and purple fluids dripped from the suit. The rancid smell visibly lifted off of the suit. Green fumes of pure horror floated into the sky. The hero crouched at the base of the tree and started doing crunches, which he did for the next month. Push-ups occupied the month after. Unfortunately, he never learned how to do push-ups, so they were embarrassingly bad, but they still helped.

As he trained, he started to remember how to use his powers. As each power returned, it caused his brain to momentarily shut off and restarted like an old computer. Once the fans were spinning and the rusted harddrive came back to life, so did he.

Once Onion Man overcame his final episode, he sat naked on the sand with his feet splashing in the water. His suit was still airing out, but there was no breeze strong enough to overcome the odor clinging to the armpits of the spandex.

A fish, no larger than a pineapple, swam up to the shore near Onion Man's splashing feet. The seafood's golden scales cast a beautiful light right into the hero's eyeballs. The fish popped his head out of the water and said, "Hey, Onion Man." The hero looked at it despite the sunlight in his eyes. "I have a message for you."

"Alright dolphin, what is it?" asked the intelligent hero.

"Delicalopolis needs you. Ice Man is being mean. People are saying it was better when you destroyed things while you tried to help. He's just freezing things and making peoples' food cold. Nobody can enjoy a warm pizza. It's become the worst place on Earth. They need a hero," said the fish.

A smile crept onto Onion Man's face. It was the ugliest smile that has come from a beautiful face. It was truly hard to believe such a hideous smile could be placed on the chiseled jaw of the handsomest, smelliest hero. He jumped into the air and took off flying to Delicalopolis.

Onion Man turned around and flew back to the island. He jumped into his suit before flying off again. Within five minutes he was back on the borders of the delicate city. Onion Man hovered heroically while he took some deep breaths. His eyes started to sting from the fumes coming off of his suit. With one more deep breath in his super lungs, the hero took off for City Hall.

The Emperor of Delicalopolis, as Ice Man called himself, sat patiently on the steps of City Hall. All of the city's citizens were gathered below, but nobody would listen to him anymore. Ice Man took a deep breath in and choked.

"What is that foul smell?" asked Ice Man.

"Onion Man is back," cheered the crowd.

Ice Man took off skating towards Onion Man. The hero flew straight down into the villain. Both men went through the road and into the subway rails. Ice Man landed on his feet after tossing Onion Man below him. The hero's head was smashed into the tracks. The cold terrorist shot an ice ball behind his back, freezing the incoming subway in its place.

"Let's go back up where they can watch," said Ice

Man with an evil smile.

Onion Man looked at him, brushed off his suit, then flew back up through the ground and road.

A few minutes later Ice Man walked up the stairs from one of the subway stations. He started skating at Onion Man, who flew at the frigid man. The smelly hero's fist collided with Ice Man's villainous jaw, which launched him backward.

Their superhuman brawl continued until almost half of the city was destroyed. Women wept and men wailed at the shattered buildings throughout the city. Childhood memories were destroyed in the fierce battle. They stared into one another's eyes as they punched and flailed. Onion Man sweated profusely and Ice Man formed a layer of condensation.

Onion Man stopped and said, "We have no reason to fight, let's stop this and get some lunch."

"I could use a bite. I'll follow you," said Ice Man.

The two supernatural men walked to the nearest standing restaurant. They sat down at a nice romantic table for two. A waiter came up and pulled out a little notebook.

"What would you two fine men like today?" asked the waiter.

"Two chicken noodle soups, please," said Onion

Man.

"And please make sure mine is cold. Just above freezing please," said Ice Man with a smile. Maybe not, the mask still covered his face.

Soon after, the waiter returned with two bowls of soup. One bowl was steaming hot, while the other one was ice cold. Ice Man started to eat his nastily cold soup through a slot on his mask.

"Wow," said Onion Man. "You're so tough and handsome. I don't think I could ever defeat you."

"I know. Why did you even return?"

Onion Man shrugged. "A fish asked me to." He twirled his spoon in his soup.

"What?"

"Do you not know what a fish is? I can teach you. So, there is this thing called the ocean. Fish have houses inside the ocean where they raise families of strong, young lads."

"That's not right. Did you go to school?"

"What's school?"

Ice Man cleared his throat and tilted his head. "Are you serious?"

Onion Man smiled. He lifted his glass of water up. "Thank you. You too. Let's toast to friendship."

"Toasting is too warm for me. Let's just eat," said Ice Man.

Onion Man mumbled as he mocked the man across the table. He continued to stir his soup. Suddenly, Onion Man's eyes got wide and bloodshot with terror. He loudly gasped. Ice Man looked up at him.

"What is that? Stop it, quick," yelled Onion Man.

Ice Man turned to see what the commotion was. Onion Man quickly switched the two soups. Ice Man turned back around.

"Are you messing with me?"

"Sorry," said Onion Man, "I thought I saw something scary."

Ignoring Onion Man, Ice Man stuck his spoon into his soup and brought it to his mouth. For some reason, the villain did not notice the steam coming off of the soup. When the hot chicken noodle touched his tongue Ice Man's hair started to melt.

"No! You have defeated me at last, Onion Man!"

Onion Man began to laugh while Ice Man slowly melted into a puddle of purified water. The city rejoiced when the news spread. Onion Man splashed around in his nemesis's watery remains. He was like a figurative child at an inadequate swimming pool.

Later that day the mayor asked Onion Man to come for another press conference. The hero was reluctant but finally decided to go.

Once he arrived, Onion Man pushed through the crowd and slowly walked up the steps. Once he was almost to the top, the mayor said, "Today our despised hero has become the hero we all dreamed of. Still not our favorite, but he's the best we have. Let's give a big cheer to Delicalopolis' newest favorite person, Onion Man!"

The crowd cheered for hours before the mayor finally quieted them down.

"I would like to present the key to the city to Onion Man. You finally almost became the hero you always wanted to be," said the mayor.

Onion Man continued to protect Delicalopolis for the rest of his life, which is forever since he's a superhero. The city never stopped praising him for saving them from the dreaded Ice Man, until something even worse showed up in town.

Part II
The Repugnant Onion Man

A Coming of Age Story

Delicalopolis. So delicate. The buildings glowed from the beautiful orange sunset. Some colorblind Delicalopians were unimpressed and were quoted saying, "It was grey."

Citizens roamed the streets and frequently passed the handsome statue of the smelliest of all heroes. Onion Man stood heroically, made of marble, stone, granite, pudding, and chocolate chips. Each muscle was sculpted to look like the ideal man, the image all vegetables strive to resemble. The buildings destroyed in the final battle with Ice Man were half rebuilt. Fast food restaurants took the place of the most important office buildings and museums.

Rick Rabet, a reporter for the Channel Fourteen Delicate News, was walking around town inter- viewing locals about their opinions of the hero. Mr. Rabet had thick black hair that he greased back. An incredibly amazing mustache hovered over his lip. His nose, slightly upturned like a pig, was almost as big as a pelican's beak. Beautiful yellow colored eyes were buried deep in his face. His smile was simply gorgeous: Yellow, brown, and filled with holes. His smile made women cave in, break down, give in, and in some commonly rare cases - die. But a positive death caused by a handsome man like Mr. Rabet was the death that can only be achieved in dreams.

Citizen after citizen told Rick how amazing Onion Man was. He smelled horrible, but he was an almost average hero. They thought that was pretty cool. Almost average was better than grossly below average. People praised Onion Man as much as they praised laxatives, and some people were crazy laxative fanatics. Neither Onion Man nor the little brown pellets in the toilets of Delicalopolis' citizens smelled worse than the other. In some situations, both have also saved many lives.

Mr. Rabet, that devilishly handsome man, interviewed every person that would talk to him around town with the single goal of finding an individual with a less than content-filled opinion of the hero. He spent most of the day talking to people, but he failed to find anyone who was willing to speak out against Onion Man.

Angered by his lack of finding Onion-filled hatred, Mr. Rabet returned home late in the night. He performed his nightly ritual of filling a glass up with milk, then drinking half of the glass alone at his dinner table. His sorrow-filled tears watered down and replenished his drink, which he continued to drink until his tears and snot failed to fill the glass up fast enough to keep some substance inside the drinking apparatus.

But that night differed from the others. While Rick Rabet, the inconceivably gorgeous reporter, prepared his exquisite glass of milk, an accident occurred. The bitter man was too distracted with his hatred and sorrow to notice that he grabbed an old bottle of hazardous toxic waste from the refrigerator instead of his half gallon of 1% milk. Mr. Rabet did not notice the sickly green glow that bathed his face in radiation as he poured the waste from the rusted metal container. He cried and he drank.

He continued to cry and drink for hours upon hours until the sun rose and the mail persons delivered piles of junk mail. The waste seeped out of his intestines and sank into Mr. Rabet's skin, turning it into a thick exoskeleton-like hide. While he slept away his agony, Rick continued to transform. He grew tendrils of smoky gray hair out of the thick hide and his ears sagged along his face. Teeth rotted and turned to dust inside the reporter's mouth until only four jagged chompers remained at the front of his mouth. A chunk of hide and fur sprouted near his butt.

When Rick Rabbet awoke later that day, he woke up as the *Rabid Rabbit*.

Flying faster than a skunk can run, Onion Man propelled himself through the air with superpowers and flatulence. Delicalopolis stood brilliantly in the sun's creepy gaze. The only crime that happened since Ice Man's fall was the occasional high school kid who thought he could shoplift. Three years in prison, thanks to Onion Man, quickly taught them a lesson.

The city was beautiful and peaceful. The vegetable-scented man floated around, watching children and old ladies, protecting the innocent lives of millions. Millions of old ladies. One hero never thought he would need to help so many elderly women cross the street, but Onion Man took the task with pride.

No city in the world had ever been as peaceful as Delicalopolis was, but the happy citizens realized that the peace came with a smelly cost.

Onion Man, the hero of all heroes, swam through the stench of the street, unopposed and fearless. Nobody had challenged Onion Man, making him feel stronger than invincible.

He stopped, perching himself atop a stoplight pole hanging over a busy intersection. The drivers below quickly rolled up their windows. The hero waved in the style of a beauty queen, unaware of the fact that ordinary people do not wave in such a fashion. The people below ignored him and continued with their hurried commutes, only to get stuck in traffic a quarter of a mile down the road.

Onion Man's original lime green suit had faded and rotted away, leaving a crusty husk of a suit somewhere between gray and vomit colors. It formed an unnecessary exoskeleton around the muscular, and somewhat overweight, superhero. Onion Man's training regimen had plummeted with the lack of competition or threat to his beloved city. Not that he normally trained often, but he made an effort to train even less than normal. A belly, like a potbelly pig, had begun to bulge from the abdomen of the very fit, very slim hero. His manly jaw remained sculpted and impressively angled, but his torso no longer fit the supermodel standards.

On top of the light pole, Onion Man surveyed the town, scanning the areas of known crime where there had not been a crime in weeks. He wasn't sure what to do with his time when there wasn't crime to fight, but the criminals knew better than to compete against the hero because one punch would shatter their rib cage and collapse their lungs.

As Onion Man focused on the conveniently named Alleyway of Mugging, he felt a presence in the distance behind him. A furry creature hopped across the road. His senses told him it was only a rabbit, an average hare. He spun as eloquently as a dancer on a single toe, expertly balancing himself high above the intersection. The hero couldn't see any sign of the creature that had moved behind him. Onion Man wasn't aware if it was a rabbit or a monster. Either way, he wanted to eat it, and his rumbling stomach had long ago given up the idea of surrender.

Filled with cravings for delectable meats and juicy innards, Onion Man jumped off the light pole. As he neared the pavement, a taxi drove beneath him. He broke through the roof and landed perfectly in the back seat.

"Onward steed," commanded Onion Man.

The taxi driver, far too afraid to argue with Onion Man, nodded and stomped on the gas pedal. Smoke drifted in the air behind the vehicle as the rubber burnt off the tires. Fear overtook the driver, forcing him to close his eyes and scream. Incoming traffic swerved to dodge the speeding taxi, but a driver of a large truck had also felt the need to close his eyes and scream. The vehicles collided. Onion Man, without a seatbelt to constrain him, was catapulted through the windshield and over two blocks of buildings. He plummeted into the asphalt of the road, raining debris onto the pedestrians passing by.

Onion Man's impenetrable body was undamaged, but his feelings were mildly hurt. He dragged himself out of the small crater in the center of the road and stretched his arms above his head until the stench of his armpits reached his nose. A quick shake of his head dispelled the overwhelming smell.

He smiled and surveyed the area. His eyes locked onto a furry silhouetted form at the end of the street. Onion Man carefully positioned his feet into a wide stance that made him do a partial squat. There was no doubt that he looked incredibly tough. Behind the hero, a conveniently placed spotlight turned on and illuminated the Rabid Rabbit. Rumbling continued in his stomach as the insatiable hunger thought of the delicate flesh of a rabbit.

"May I please eat you?" Onion Man knew being polite was always an important part of any conversation. The rabbit's response was to leap at him. Rick's incredible mutated strength brought him directly in front of Onion Man in a single bound. It startled the hero, causing him to stumble back into the crater.

"You ruined my life." Rick's voice was pitchy at best. He would never make it as a singer or public speaker. His television days were definitely behind him.

Onion Man climbed back out and poked the rabbit in the chest. "I don't even know you." The hero's visibly smelly breath drifted through the air and seeped into Rick's nostrils, surprising and partially paralyzing the monstrous rabbit. He flinched and fell over in a fight for clean air. The reaction to his breath surprised Onion Man, so he breathed into his hand and smelled it. Despite his breath being an unhealthy green, he thought he had smelled much worse, and therefore didn't need a breath mint or his monthly teeth brushing (which was two days away).

"Are you a supervillain or something?" Onion Man squatted down to look Rick in the eyes.

"Obviously," wheezed Rick, still fighting for air. He brought his enormous feet up and kicked the smelly man with all his strength. Onion Man was thrown through the air, passing over the car wreck he had come from, and landed two miles down the road. Before the hero fully recovered to his feet, the Rabid Rabbit landed before him and kicked him to the other side of town. This pattern went on for several hours, making the two men the new record holders for destroying the most roads within a given day.

City officials sat inside and cried while eating ice cream as they knew incredibly dense piles of paperwork were going to follow the super-powered brawl happening outside.

With each consecutive kick, Onion Man was reminded that his poor fitness had lowered his reaction times. There was no fear that he may be killed by the rabbit, but he would not be able to defeat the villain until he could fight back. Being kicked so much made Onion Man feel insecure about his body and his heroic deeds. Was he a hero or a pathetic repugnant invincible flying man that couldn't defeat a school child? He wasn't sure.

How would Onion Man defeat this new villain? How would he make it home in time for dinner? How many questions could he ask?

Onion Man plummeted back to the ground. The road exploded into a cloud of dust and the hero struggled back to his feet. The Rabid Rabbit landed beside Onion Man and coughed.

"Where are you?" he asked through a scratchy throat.

"Here," shouted Onion Man.

"Oh," Rick scratched his head. "Thank you." He jumped into the smoke and launched the vegetable hero straight into the air.

Onion Man floated above a cloud, undecided if we would start flying or not. Pros and Cons lists always help in these types of situations. Start with the pros, he decided. No hitting the ground, no more rabbit kicks, a nice breeze.

Some cons? Well, flying does take a good amount of effort. Onion Man nodded to himself. It did take some effort. More than he'd like.

Then it struck him.

An unsuspecting pigeon right to the forehead. It dropped, lifeless from severe head trauma.

Poor pigeon, thought Onion Man as he also plummeted through the air. It briefly looked like the bird was still alive because they both fell at the same rate.

"What an interesting observation," said Onion Man. "I wonder how the science works for us two to fall at the same rate."

Now, who he was talking to was a mystery. First, his voice couldn't be heard over the roaring of the wind. Second, and most important, the bird was super dead. It was unable to hear, based on the deadness.

During the time between collision with the bird and collision with the ground, the hero decided he would commission a sculpture of this bird, which he just decided to call Jimothy.

The same baker/sculpture that created his piece would have the opportunity to create another such statue. It would become a new tourist attraction. Who wouldn't love the Jimothy Pigeon statue?

Then it struck him. Again.

Pavement, then a car, then an airplane that was using the highway as a runway. Onion Man had flashbacks to the last time he was a speedbump. He didn't enjoy it then. This time it was like a massage from a dinosaur. Weirdly pleasant.

He continued to lie in the onion crater. As a brief pause from daily life, if not as an excuse to hide from the rabbit.

"I can't beat him," said Onion Man, once again not to anyone specific. "I should run away and train."

As the words left his chapped lips, the realization came that he had done the exact thing against Ice Man. But the new, strong Onion Man didn't run and cry like the old version. The new, upgraded hero stood up to bullies and cried in their faces.

Onion Man stood and flexed all the fat in his stomach to his butt cheeks and biceps, which gave a weird idea that he should be a model after his hero days are over.

His crusty, old suit exploded off his muscular, new body. The naked vegetable-man stood in the streets, averting all the gazes of drivers from the road to his shining body. It was a historic day because this specific incident caused the largest traffic pileup in Delicalopolis history.

One vehicle involved in this event was a semi-truck hauling seven tons of leeks. Because all eyes were on Onion Man's onions, the driver could not turn his gaze or his steering wheel.

The fight between hero and villain had already caused so much damage throughout the day. So, a little more wouldn't hurt.

Onion Man was once again launched through several buildings, cheeks on both ends flapping through the wind. After passing through the third building, he flexed again, forcing the fat to travel to his bottom. The extra padding acted like a spring and launched him backward. He landed in front of the semi-truck, which was on fire.

He stared at the wreckage, trying to pull an idea out of his brain. Did his onion powers have a way to put out fire? A chilling breath left his lips.

"Is this ice breath?" he thought.

The cold air quickly vanished, unable to put out the flames. Onion Man swished his salvia around in his mouth, gathering mucous and bits of food in an ever-growing ball. He was sure it was enough to extinguish the fire.

In one big effort, he spat the ball towards the flaming truck. The water sizzled and evaporated.

The hero was once again out of ideas.

"Can you please help?" asked the driver. He was a small man with a large head.

"I'm working on it."

Onion Man ripped the door off the passenger side and climbed into the truck. He grabbed the driver's hands.

"Can you think of any powers to put out the fire?"

"No, but can you just pull me out quick instead?"

Onion Man shook his head. It simply wasn't an option. "I'm sorry, sir. The only way to help is—"

The road shook like an earthquake struck.

"I have a bad feeling," said the driver.

"Is it because I'm naked?" asked Onion Man.

The driver shrugged. Nudity wasn't his main concern. Growling sounded from outside the truck, drawing closer with each shake of the road. Onion Man squeezed the driver's hands a bit tighter.

"Don't panic."

The Rabid Rabbit grabbed Onion Man's neck and threw him as far as he could. Unfortunately for the driver, the hero never let go of his hands. The two men were flying through the air. Onion Man for the hundredth time that day, and a lifetime first for the driver.

Onion Man pulled him close to comfort him, but the driver felt anything but comfortable. They crashed into the cobblestones next to Onion Man's statue. The driver, perfectly unharmed, stood and ran. The smelly hero stood and took a deep breath. He shifted into a fighting stance that he had seen in an old martial arts movie. Rick was flying through the air, about to crash like a meteor.

Delicalopolis's protector wasn't scared of anything. He was called a superhero for a reason, and he was set on proving himself to himself.

Onion Man kicked forward and was amazed by his timing. The top of his foot struck between Rick's legs as the rabbit monster landed. The force of the kick shot Rick right back into the air. Unseen civilians cheered.

Onion Man's foot ached from the hit, but he was proud to feel the pain. He squinted and looked into the sky. The Rabid Rabbit was nowhere to be seen.

The hero sat on the cold cobblestone and shouted, "Can someone bring me a pizza?"

A gangly man ran out a short time later with a fresh cheese pizza. Onion Man sat, somewhat reclined, beside the statue of himself and ate the entirety of the mediocre pizza.

After he finished eating, he stretched and glanced back into the sky. Still, no sign of the villain.

"Guess I'll go pick up a new suit," said Onion Man to the empty pizza box.

He ran at lightning speeds back to his apartment on the other side of town. While he had better control over many of his powers, there were a few he hadn't yet mastered. The running took him straight through his door. Wood splintered and exploded throughout the room inside.

The interior of his apartment was already quite messy. Unacceptably messy for the average person, but heroes all have different standards. For another hero, Onion Man's apartment may have been too clean. Who is to say? Food wrappers and soda bottles littered the floor and cobwebs hung from the corners of the walls. The paint itself thought it was ugly with a color somewhere between mustard and hot pink.

"This is gross," said Onion Man.

"Yeah, it is," said a cockroach.

Onion Man stepped on the cockroach and tiptoed through the living room. A bright orange spandex suit hung from a hook in the closet.

"Why did I ever order an orange suit?" he mumbled to himself. It took most of his strength to stretch the suit over his body. The suit snapped into place and revealed more than a decent person would show, but it was better than nudity while flying around.

With the extra compression and lack of blood flowing to his brain, Onion Man felt ready to defeat any enemy. Even if the Rabid Rabbit never fell back to Earth.

Reconstruction efforts began immediately around Delicalopolis. Onion Man felt empowered, reawoken after his brief brawl. He wanted to help in any way he could. The mayor passed out gas masks to all construction workers as a precaution.

The invincible hero lifted bricks and stones, poured concrete, and carried forklifts. Construction moved quickly with all his extra help, but a new job was also created.

Onion Man had his arms raised for so long that birds were dropping from the sky. A new position,

Bird Sweeper, was filled with ten able-bodied workers that cleaned up the poor, dead birds.

Onion Man worked hard, unaware of his accidental avicide. He worked harder than he had ever worked before. He even ended up sweeping an old lady's driveway.

The citizens of Delicalopolis had never doubted Onion Man since his defeat of Ice Man. His new effort and enthusiasm were very appreciated. Before the sunset that day, they managed to patch up the buildings ruined earlier and rebuild some from the fight with Ice Man. Onion Man did most of the work and realized he had other career opportunities if being a hero grows old. He wasn't even the smelliest man at the construction site.

He actually was. He just didn't think he was.

Peace returned to Delicalopolis. A calmness fell over the city as Onion Man flew around, watching for trouble. He felt like a large pumpkin, but still just as much of a hero.

Kids waved as he flew overhead, and sometimes he waved back. This new peace lasted for a whole twelve hours.

Sonic booms shattered all the windows across Delicalopolis as a fireball fell from the sky. It crashed in the city center and sent debris above the tallest buildings. Onion Man was showered with pebbles, which caused him to lose control. He fell into the new crater and crashed beside the mysterious object.

It looked like a toaster for the biggest bread slices in the world and it hummed like an irradiated flute.

Steam shot out all around the object as one of its walls lowered itself to the ground. A sickly green light bathed the inside, revealing the Rabid Rabbit. But something was different about him. Notably, the alien-looking armor and dripping plasma sword.

Onion Man brushed dirt and pebbles off his suit. The green glow with his orange suit was really unflattering, so he was a bit bummed about that.

"Hey, you're alive," said Onion Man. "I was worried about you."

The Rabbit growled and ran at Onion Man. The hero didn't understand the situation. He understood very little. When the villain swung his new plasma sword, Onion Man didn't try to dodge or block. He was invincible. Why put in the extra work when only words can hurt you?

The blade sliced right through Onion Man's layered flesh, and his right arm dropped to the ground. A smell of caramelized vegetables spread through the air.

They both looked at his arm lying in the dirt. Onion Man bent down and picked up his dismembered arm. He held it near the elbow and slapped Rick Rabet.

"That was incredibly rude," said Onion Man.

He stuck his arm back into place. The skin stitched itself back together, but he was unable to move it.

"It looks like it half worked," he said.

"Then I'll make your whole body half work," said the Rabid Rabbit. He growled and charged Onion Man again.

Onion Man slapped the villain as Rick managed to also slice off the hero's left arm. The villain was thrown back into the toaster, and the hero bent down and rolled on the ground until he was able to reconnect his arm. Now, he had two arms that he could not move.

"Don't ruin my spaceship," said Rick as he crawled back out of the green light.

"It's a spaceship? I thought it was a toaster."

Rick walked toward the hero, each step shaking the ground.

"How did the citizens of Delicalopolis get so unlucky to have you as their hero? You are the worst excuse for a superhero."

A tear ran down Onion Man's smooth, manly cheek. His arms already felt funny, and now his heart did too.

"How cruel can you be?" asked Onion Man.

"Enough," said Rick as he swung his sword.

Onion Man, unable to wiggle his appendages, headbutt the incoming blade. That moment, they both discovered the hero's skull was stronger than space plasma. Rick's alien weapon broke and dripped into a puddle of plasma at their feet. His weird, rabbit eyes grew twice as large and opened wider than ever before. He was horrified.

Onion Man was also horrified. Rick's mutated eyes were super gross. Like the grossest thing he had ever seen. So gross that he had to say something.

"Dude, your eyes are literally disgusting." Onion Man never intended to be cruel in any way. He only ever wanted to help the people of Delicalopolis. Luckily, he was too socially unaware to realize that Rick Rabet's feelings had never been more hurt.

Rick became a villain out of a dislike of the smelly hero, but now he harbored a deeper hatred for the super-powered man he saw as a bully. The words that came from Onion Man scarred Rick more deeply than the kick that sent him to space.

The Rabid Rabbit pressed a button on his fancy space armor and the humming sound returned in the air. Wires snaked out and wrapped around his body, forming layer upon layer of machinery. It was a slow process, but Onion Man didn't attempt to stop Rick's evolution. More wires appeared, seemingly from nowhere until the armor suit was four times the size of Onion Man.

The Rabid Rabbit became the *Mecha Lagomorph*.

"I, the Mecha Lagomorph, will destroy you." Rick's voice now sounded slightly robotic, which Onion Man thought made sense with all the wires and such.

"I have to admit your new name doesn't scare me in the same way," said the hero.

"Then I will use actions instead of words."

A big robo rabbit fist punched Onion Man. His unusable arms once again detached and stayed within the crater. The rest of Onion Man was sent into space.

The first thing he noticed was the lack of sound. It was unsettling and his head hurt. The hero took a deep breath and felt more relaxed with lungs full of vacuum and all the silence in the world.

He slowly floated, feeling the gravity of Earth pulling on him, but not showing any interest in listening to it. His gaze drifted around until he found the sun. It was hard to miss. Surprisingly, the sun was super bright. Not surprising, Onion Man stared right at it. For like, a really long time.

A normal person wouldn't be able to see anything after such an event. What kind of person would stare at the sun?

Meanwhile, back on Earth...

The Mecha Lagomorph still stood in the crater with Onion Man's arms. He was happy to get revenge for getting kicked into space.

But he was slightly concerned that Onion Man would meet the same aliens that gave him all the fancy technology. At the same time, he knew Onion Man would be too dumb to use anything they gave him.

He used his weird eyes to scan the sky. No sign of the hero. Should he wait? Rick had never been a patient person. Now that he was a mutant and a cyborg, he had less patience than ever before. He slowly climbed out of the crater, carefully placing each step. Just because he was a giant mech villain didn't mean he couldn't slip or fall.

Nobody stood around in the city center. They fled when the toaster fell from the sky. A weak breeze blew through the city, which had fallen silent. It was rather uncomfortable. Onion Man's smell cleared and left the city smelling of wet socks.

"Is this what the city's normal smell is?" thought Rick.

Did other cities smell of socks? Many questions were proposed without any answers. Rick stomped through town, leaving giant rabbit footprints in the asphalt with each step. That was going to ruin many commutes.

The villain walked through town, weaving up and down side streets and main thoroughfares. He was growing tired, and each step fell heavier than the last. Employees of the Department of Transportation tracked Rick and cried as they saw his path of destruction. A handful of employees started the paperwork they knew would be needed at a later date.

Mecha Lagomorph was growing bored. Unsure of when, or if, Onion Man would return. What would he do without the hero? He was a mutant cyborg bunny now, and he assumed correctly that news stations weren't ready to hire such a creature. Wind blew down the street, stirring up the tiniest pieces of rubble. The breeze felt cool against Rick's robo tears, which were normal tears on his metal face.

Onion Man, still staring into the sun, was on fire.

Very literally.

He had been burning for about half an hour. It wasn't comfortable, but it also wasn't unpleasant. To him, it was like that perfect temperature in the shower where you know it's too hot, but it also feels nice so you keep it there. His suit, conveniently being a similar color to the burning gas of the sun, was able to withstand the intense heat and general burning.

A deep breath filled his lungs with fire, and he momentarily felt like a dragon, which he wasn't. Because he's a vegetable-based man hero.

Another deep breath pulled all the fire from the outside of his body into his lungs and he held it there. It felt weird having lungs filled with vacuum and fire simultaneously, but he did it anyway.

Onion Man felt as if he had been reborn from the fire. Rejuvenated and awake for the first time in his life. New arms sprouted from his shoulders and quickly grew to their full size. He didn't even know he had such a power.

Should he change his name? The thought crossed his mind. What would it be?

Phoenix man?

Stargazer?

Fire Man? That one seemed too similar to his past villain.

Delicalopolis's citizens wouldn't want to call him anything else. They were set on their hero now. He knew that. But he could call himself a new name, especially when he talked in the third person.

"Fried Onion," he whispered to himself, letting the fire wheeze out of his mouth.

The thought of a dragon-based name never crossed his mind. It wouldn't have been fitting anyway, but most people would think of a dragon while exhaling fire.

Fried Onion took another deep breath and relaxed. His eyes closed and he let gravity pull him down. Flames danced in the blackness of his mind and his fat burned away.

Gravity brought him back into the atmosphere quickly. Faster than he could normally move. Fried Onion opened his eyes and rotated into his normal flying pose. His whole body was still on fire as he flew through the sky. Many people mistook him for a meteor, which also would have been a better name.

There were plenty of ways the hero could have slowed down when he was above Delicalopolis. He had powers that let him stop and hover. He had his butt bouncing abilities. He even had strong enough arms to grab onto something and stop.

Did he do any of those things?

Fried Onion continued moving at over 100,000 miles per hour until he hit the ground. He didn't choose to slow down, but the ground decided it would be a good idea.

The crater, just a few hundred feet from the edge of Delicalopolis, was enormous. Fried Onion stood at the bottom, staring into the sky. It would make a great lake later if he could find a way to bring enough water. Maybe he would crash from space a few more times to create a nice series of pools.

Now that he was back on Earth, Fried Onion was realizing that his new name was a bit lame. Onion Man was much cooler. He would spend the rest of the day deciding which he would use.

The hero stood, stretched, peed, and flew out of the crater. Discomfort bubbled in his stomach as he hovered over his delicate city. Footsteps marred the beautiful landscape of streets, pollution, and overpopulation. Mecha Lagomorph's heavy steps had paced around the entire city, and Fried Onion Man felt like he would out-weep a newborn in a crying contest.

What could be done?

"Are you going to beat him?" asked a weirdly placed small child.

Onion Man looked around for the source of the voice. A short, wiry boy stood atop the tallest arcade.

"What are you doing up there, boy?"

The child looked around. Tears welled up in his eyes.

"I'm looking at all the destruction. You abandoned us, Onion Man." The child's voice was shaky.

He was clearly trying to hold back his tears, but Onion Man was an expert crier. He wasn't even aware that you could hold back tears.

"I didn't abandon anyone, little thing. I was simply powering up. It is my time to get revenge on this monstrous creature."

The child gave him a thumbs up and said no more. It was good too because Onion Man wasn't planning on saying anything else.

"Where hath the creature gone?" asked Onion Man.

Nobody responded because nobody was around. Even the little child mysteriously vanished. Super hearing pulled sound waves into his ear. So many waves entered that he felt like he heard the whole world. Earthworms below the city dug and munched on dirt and it was the most obnoxious sound he had ever encountered. He was a hero to the people, but he would have happily been a villain to all the hungry worms crawling around.

The flap of bird wings, wind slowly eroding stones, and even his suit chafing against his skin filled the entirety of his consciousness.

"It'll be impossible to find him with all these distractions," said Onion Man.

Saying anything was a really dumb idea. With his super-hearing activated, each word muttered from his lips sounded like a bulldozer driving over his face while six planes took off simultaneously.

Onion Man cried and curled into a fetal position. He wept buckets worth of salty, smelly tears. The hero sobbed like a freshly birthed newborn.

"Cool, you're back," came a robotic-sounding voice from above.

Onion Man looked up at Rick's mutated robo face. His vision was quickly obscured by a big mech foot pushing him into the ground.

"Rude," said Onion Man, but his voice was muffled by the large foot. Being stomped into the ground was uncomfortable, so Fried Onion stood up. He still hadn't decided on which name would fit him best. Likely Onion Man, as that was his original name and the only one anyone else would know him by. On the other hand, Fried Onion conveyed the life-changing experience he had only minutes before while in space. The discussion for which would be a better fit would continue to be debated throughout history. It was a main topic for philosophy students at the University of Delicalopolis, which has not been founded yet.

Onion Man's incredible ability to stand up sent Mecha Lagomorph straight into the air as if the vegetable hero was a catapult, which he was not.

Luckily for Rick, his new machinery added an extra couple thousand pounds. He found his way back to the ground rapidly and used his new weight to crush Onion Man.

Luckily for Onion Man, he was uncrushable.

Instead, the two found themselves in a weird cheerleading-type position of Rick standing on Onion Man's shoulders. A weird sense of friendship, like that of a bond with a teammate, coursed through the two men. They both had never felt closer to another living being than they did at that moment.

Was this the end of their conflict?

Had they resolved their differences with a shoulder stand?

Onion Man added *Cheerleader* to the growing list of other potential occupations in his mind.

Rick looked down at the hero's beautiful blonde hair. It was a great mane, he thought. The tear-filled irradiated milk cocktail in his stomach started to gurgle.

Simply indigestion. Right? Couldn't be anything else since the rest of his body was mechanical.

But Rick's hatred of the hero resurfaced as the contents of his stomach found more than one serviceable exit from the mechanical body of Rick Rabet.

Toxic waste, milk, and tears ejected themselves from the front and rear of the Lagomorph villain. Onion Man bathed in the chemicals dropped from Rick.

Somehow, Onion Man didn't smell any worse than normal. In fact, he may have even smelled slightly better after Rick released his liquidy waste upon the hero.

Mecha Lagomorph looked below at the poop-covered hero and felt his renewed rage course through his wires. He began stomping on Onion Man's shoulders, slowly pounding him into the ground like a big vegetable nail.

Onion Man wasn't a fan of that. He didn't even know how to properly use a hammer. Images of his time in space flickered through his mind. He felt Fried Onion reemerge.

Fire emerged from Onion Man's shoulders and thighs. Red and orange flames danced and continued to climb his body. Rick continued stomping but felt more like he was trying to walk through a muddy path. His eyes drifted down, where he saw his mutated rabbit feet exposed. The metal had melted away onto Onion Man, forming a chest plate of armor for the hero.

"My feet are on your chest," yelled Rick.

Fried Onion ignored him. He was done listening to his heart. He was ready to destroy the Rabbit.

Onion Man's fist flew up, hit Rick between the legs, and launched him straight into the air once again. He felt powerful, which was good because he was rather powerful.

Onion Man watched the clear sky as Rick flew up and vanished. The hero was happy the sun was out. It was rather pleasant. The sun had been out for the last few weeks, which was a nice change from the previous month where it rained almost every other day. Meteorologists had gotten bored of telling everyone it was going to rain. They didn't enjoy it.

But somebody had to tell the people when it was going to rain, or else someone would have ended up outside without an umbrella or a raincoat. The weather people would have been responsible for that, and they couldn't handle having that on their conscience.

Onion Man noticed a dog walking past. There was not an owner in sight, but the dog didn't seem bothered or worried. They made eye contact for a weirdly long time. Like their souls intertwined and held hands. It felt weird. Super weird. Onion Man wasn't even sure what he was feeling after the extended eye contact, but he knew he was in some way changed. The little bichon continued its walk down the sidewalk, seemingly unaffected by this life-altering event.

Rick was on his way back to the ground. He wasn't in a great mood. His arch-enemy, Onion Man, was really hitting his buttons. Not literally, since he had buttons now. But there was a chance Onion Man would both literally and figuratively hit his buttons. He hoped it would be one or the other. Either way, he wanted to finish this fight and not have either of them launched into the air again.

Below, Onion Man also decided it was time to end things. He flexed, squeezed, and wiggled all of the muscles in his body. His brain grew and pressed against his skull, his tongue wriggled in his throat, and his buttcheeks danced beneath his spandex suit.

His whole body hurt from flexing so hard, but it was time to unleash the oil in this Fried Onion.

Flames like an illegal bonfire erupted from the oily hero. Heat comparable to the sun's own radiated off the hero and began melting his surroundings.

Rick continued his fall and felt the overwhelming heat as he neared the ground. The road was melted into molten lava almost instantly, and the metal form around the Rabid Rabbit dripped from him like cheap chocolate.

Onion Man smiled, feeling the heat on his little teeth, as he watched Rick, the Rabid Rabbit and Mecha Lagomorph, plummet straight into the pool of lava.

Both of them wanted the fight to end. And so, it did. It was more brutal than Onion Man wanted, and less favorable than Rick wanted.

Citizens of Delicalopolis started to emerge from the buildings and rubble. Many had watched from the safety of cover, silently cheering on their unstoppable hero. It would have been too dangerous to watch in the open. One man was even crushed as he emerged from the rubble of a building. That's why you wear hard hats at construction sites.

Cheering exploded from all around. It filled the whole city and made Onion Man smile his biggest smile yet. He unflexed and let the fire die out. Unfortunately, the ground beneath his feet was also melted, and it all rapidly cooled. Onion Man now felt like a statue, unable to move his feet. Citizens continued walking closer, cheering and screaming the whole way.

He started to feel uncomfortable from the praise. Mostly because several hundred people were quickly surrounding him. Even with super strength, he could be overwhelmed rather swiftly.

"Please don't kill me," he mumbled over and over hoping they wouldn't kill him.

When they got close, a few construction workers stepped forward and used sledgehammers to break the igneous rock trapping his feet.

"Thank you," said the hero.

"No, thank you," said a couple of hundred citizens simultaneously.

That made him more uncomfortable than anything else that had ever happened.

Onion Man, feet freed, floated into the air and waved at the people. "I'll be off," he said. "I'll return when the next villain arrives."

"What if there isn't a next villain?" asked the dog from earlier.

"Then I'll become a cheerleader."

Nobody was quite sure why. But they didn't need to know. Onion Man knew why deep in his heart and even deeper in his swollen brain.

Part III
The Rancid Onion Man

A Dystopian YA Novel

What was the first thing you remember when you entered Delicaloplis? I remember the smell, as many do. It hits you like a baseball bat to the forehead. Eye-watering, foul, gut-wrenching air hanging above the streets. The smell is almost visible in a green aura around the citizens.

It is called a delicate city, but why? Its people are more resilient than cockroaches. The buildings have been rebuilt so many times, there could be philosophy books written about if they're still the same building or not. Everything about Delicalopolis screams *tough*. Especially Onion Man.

The hero of 1,000 smells. Stinkiest of all heroes. Multilayered crybaby. There are many names you could call him by, but none of them ever mentions that smile. His beautiful teeth, shining in the sunlight. Wind brushing his blonde mane over his shoulders. Visible stink flowing from his armpits.

What is there to not love about the famous Onion?

Three years went by without any sign of the hero or even the smallest crime within the borders of Delicalopolis. Even the unruly youngsters were scared to shoplift because they never knew when the smelly man would return. What if he was watching from afar, waiting for someone to become a criminal?

The city flourished in those years. People from around the world came to visit or live, especially after the eye-watering smell cleared out to a more manageable level. It still smelled. Oh, did it smell ripe. But the smell lessened to the level "Freshly Opened Septic Tank" when it was originally the level of "I'm About To Die From The Smell, Please Give Me A Gas Mask Immediately Before I Die, Oh Please Help Me". Delicalopolis became a tourist attraction with a small Onion Man museum. They even sold millions of shirts that said "The Delicate City". Tours were given through his apartment. After the hero abandoned his home, the carpets fossilized and petrified from the smell. It was dangerous to enter, so waivers were signed by each guest and they received a free tetanus shot on their way out.

Efforts to clean Delicalopolis quickly made it the greenest city on Earth. The city council even made a plan to use Onion Man's odor as a source of fuel if he ever returns. This idea drew scientists and engineers to new labs built in the city center. It became a weird hub for all types of people.

There were other theories about Onion Man as well. One guessed he was an alien who returned to space. A few even said he was a solar flare that returned to the sun. Nobody listened to those people. What a terrible theory.

Others thought he possibly rotted away like all onions do after some time. Or maybe he went back to his family. The natives of Delicalopolis knew he moved there many years ago, but they never knew where he came from.

There was also a surprising amount of people that guessed he was secretly Swedish and returned to his foreign homeland. This theory raised concerns and caused a detailed investigation by the FBI and Homeland Security. A superhero punching people through buildings was acceptable, but a foreign hero? That crossed the line, and they never allowed that line to be crossed.

Everyone was wrong. The hero rented a small cottage in the woods where it felt like winter year-round. How he rented it is a mystery because he was never once paid for his heroic efforts. How he paid his apartment's rent for so many years is also a mystery that will likely remain unsolved.

In this cottage, Onion Man dedicated his time to reading, writing, and photography. Thoughts of changing jobs never left his mind, and his time off from heroic activities helped cement the idea of finding a new career.

Any danger in Delicalopolis would immediately set off an alarm deep within Onion Man's brain, so he wasn't concerned with what was happening in the city. He wasn't sure how he knew the city was safe, but he was confident in his instincts.

There was no time in his past that Onion Man had encountered a book he was willing to read. This left him severely unsuited to choosing a book. When he first moved out to the woods, he brought a stack of books to start with.

The first book he read was a dictionary. He didn't understand the story, but it still managed to engage him throughout the time it took him to finish. A thesaurus was the next book he grabbed, thinking it was a sequel to the dictionary.

This continued for some time with him picking up encyclopedias and books of literary theory. While he enjoyed the activity of reading, he couldn't understand why some people did it with so much excitement. It wasn't until he found a book about a snail going on an adventure to find its dad that Onion Man found the joy of reading.

"What if I wrote my own story?" he thought aloud to himself three years ago.

Now, three years later, Onion Man was polishing his masterpiece: *The Delicate Man*.

It was, of course, a memoir. Onion Man found his own story interesting enough that he wanted to write it down. He did struggle with writing, and after three years of drafts and rewrites, Onion Man found himself with less than one page of writing.

The Delicate Man

When I was seven, I started to smell. It never ended. I still smell. I was friends with a turtle and then I went to the city called Delicalopolis. I cried a lot because people yelled at me until I melted a cold guy. Then I melted a big bunny. I am a hero.

While it is unclear how this story would be received, both critically and commercially, it was a fair assumption to say it isn't a great story.

It was almost as if Onion Man forgot most of his own story. Possibly from a few too many kicks and too many walls broken through. The important thing is that Onion Man tried a new profession. He clearly was not meant to be a writer or even a scholar in any form.

Without any doubt, Onion Man was meant to be a hero. Mostly because he was never even given a proper name. What if we called him Earl? Or maybe Eugene?

Other names didn't matter because it was time for the legendary hero to return to work. While Onion Man was staring at his paragraph-long memoir, an unknown object appeared over Delicalopolis.

All it did was hover, but Onion Man felt an unease deep in his stomach and a throbbing deep in his brain. He grabbed his laptop and threw it with all his strength. It broke through the window and disappeared into the atmosphere. He hopped out the same window and started running towards his beloved city.

Meanwhile, in Delicaloplis, scientists gathered in the city center below the object. It was being referred to as an object, but realistically it was almost the same size as the city and it looked like a large basket. Almost like a monstrous picnic basket.

Astronomers, biologists, archaeologists, and other lesser-known science specialists discussed what it could possibly be.

"Clearly something from space," said an astronomer.

But what could it be? They all wondered. It looked like it was made of woven wicker, but that wouldn't hold up in the vacuum of space. That was the thought the astronomers had. The astrologists were busy trying to figure out if it was something they recognized. It surely wasn't a crab or a lion, so they gave up.

Delicalopolis fell into a silent city as each and every person watched the picnic basket in the sky. Lights of all colors flashed. It was like spotlights pointing throughout the city. A few colorblind people later reported that the basket had grey lights. Others reported there were colors they had never seen before.

The lights blinded the scientists and pseudo-scientists and caused many people to hide indoors. Less than ten minutes later, a cloud descended on the city. It looked like an ordinary cloud, but everyone who encountered it reported scents of fresh fruit, smoothies, or yogurt.

It was a pleasant, yet confusing smell that filled Delicalopolis. Some people felt uncomfortable and others were happy to push out the regular city smell. A few odd people missed the smell of body odor and onions.

Deep laughter echoed through the city, managing to reach both ears of every person. The laugh sent shivers and created nightmares for the upcoming night. During the time of peace, Delicalopolis's police department fell apart. They had nothing to do even when Onion Man was there, so they no longer went to work. And within moments, the city felt as if it was held hostage. There was no line of defense, so the whole city surrendered before even knowing if they were being attacked.

A door opened from the space basket and a metal ramp slowly extended downward to the city center. It moved at 'old lady crossing the street' speed. The scientists, engineers, and others that were curious watched the ramp inch towards them with an unrivaled sense of anticipation.

Through the lights and smoke, a vague outline of a silhouette appeared at the door. It walked down to the end of the ramp and stood with its arms crossed. The figure was shaped like a crescent moon with arms and legs.

Chatter started between the experts below.

"Is it an alien?"

"It has to be!"

"Is it my mom? What if she's angry?"

Outside the tightly knit group of scientists, engineers, and pseudoscientists, normal people made their own guesses about what the creature may be.

Anticipation waxed and waned as the sun vanished, then reappeared in the morning. The ramp continued to descend, but by morning it had reached the edge of the smoke near the city center. Everyone braced themselves and stared, eager to see what stood on the ramp.

The first thing they saw when it emerged from the smoke was the bright yellow skin. Two buggy eyes sat above a long, thin nose. Its mouth stretched the whole width of the creature in a wicked smirk.

"It's just a big banana," shouted the astrologist.

"Isn't that disappointing?" said another.

The banana uncrossed his arms and jumped from the edge of the ramp, still thirty feet in the air. It landed and cracked the cement beneath its red shoes. The banana stood about twelve feet tall.

"I am Banana Man," he shouted.

His voice, much like his laugh, was deep and discomforting.

"My friends and I have come to take over this city."

A citizen raised his hand.

"What is it?" asked Banana Man.

"Why not a different city? Or the whole world?"

Banana Man sighed. He walked up to the citizen and kicked. The citizen quickly flew into the sky and vanished.

"Any other questions?"

Nobody raised a hand.

"My friends will be here soon. For now, bring me all of your vegetables."

Everyone in the city center scattered and scurried towards their homes and grocery stores.

Many miles away, Onion Man ran. He ran across an ocean, each step on the water sent waves that would be tsunami-level by the time they reached shore. The hero was, of course, unaware of this. Flying has always been a choice, but Onion Man rarely chose to travel in that fashion. Airplanes were one of his favorite things in existence, but he was not welcome on any because of the whole odor thing. Airline representatives said something about "choking passengers", which he is certain he didn't do on purpose. He can always fly himself, but he just often forgets that's an option.

The sense of danger in his stomach continued to grow and spread, but he couldn't move any faster. His legs moved too fast to be seen and he was starting to sweat. Once the sweat collected beneath his spandex suit, it was game over for Onion Man. Odors and diseases would collect near his feet so fast that he would become a biological weapon. All he could do was risk it and continue running.

Banana Man sniffed the statue of Onion Man and pulled back.

"Chocolate?"

He pulled back his gloved fist and punched the statue so hard it started on fire and vanished. The villain climbed on top and sat in the statue's place. He grinned and lounged as terrified citizens arrived and dropped broccoli, cabbages, and carrots at his feet. All sorts of vegetables quickly piled up around the throned villain.

The scented cloud deployed by the fruit basket was blown away by the wind, leaving small pockets of fruity air. The colorful spotlights still shined brightly, frequently blinding those looking up. It was now clear to many people that the basket was some type of spaceship or carrier for Banana Man and his friends.

People carrying armfuls of vegetables shouted and tried to point at the massive ramp. With the cloud cleared, it was easy to see the four figures exiting the ship, two by two. A massive orange with long, curly hair and no nose walked beside a bunch of grapes with different faces upon each individual purple grape.

Behind those two walked a red apple with a mohawk and a green mango. The apple wore sunglasses and was chewing something so obnoxiously it could be seen from the ground.

The mango had bumps on his face, like some fruit form of acne. He looked at his feet as he walked and didn't seem interested in where he was going.

All of the fruit monsters wore white gloves on their hands and had sneakers on their feet. Despite being able to see them, the citizens of Delicalopolis had a hard time believing these creatures existed. The five of them looked like some bad joke.

They descended the long ramp, surveying the city as they went. Citizens continued piling up vegetables the whole time until the last citizen brought forth a single leek. She dropped it and took a few steps backwards.

"Is this the last of it?" asked Banana Man.

She nodded. "That should be the last vegetable in the city."

Banana Man stood. All eyes were on the villain.

In his deep, eerie voice he yelled, "If I find a single speck of vegetable in this city, I will destroy all of you."

His friends stepped off the ramp and formed a circle around the pile of vegetables. The orange raised its hands and shouted something in an unknown language. A flash of light briefly blinded everyone watching, and when their vision returned the only thing left in the circle was ash. No vegetable crumbs could be seen.

"These are my friends," said Banana Man. "You will learn to see us as your new rulers. Together, we are the *Fruit Freaks*. My friend here," he gestured with his left hand towards the orange, "is Madame Citrus, beside her is Captain Vitis, the grape master. Next, we have Dame Malus, and the youngest, Lord Mango. If you have any questions about your domination and enslavement, please submit a formal request."

"We're good," shouted a citizen. "We've been through it before."

Banana Man pointed and within the blink of an eye, Dame Malus stood before the citizen.

"I will happily submit a formal request," shouted the same citizen.

The monstrous apple patted the citizen on the head and disappeared back to the circle.

"Now, Madame Citrus will direct you to your new daily tasks." Banana Man stepped down onto the ash pile and patted the orange on the back. "She has a special job for each of you."

"What's that smell?" asked Lord Mango.

"What smell?" asked Madame Citrus.

One citizen cheered but was quickly shushed by the others. Banana Man shot glares around, but nobody moved.

"It smells terrible," said Banana Man. "We must cleanse it."

The other Fruit Freaks grunted their approval and turned their back to the center and looked out at the city. A strong breeze almost pushed the Freaks off their feet. They turned, curious to the source, and saw diced pieces of mango flying through the air. Next to Lord Mango's empty shoes stood a man with beautiful hair and breath-taking eyes.

"Onion Man is back," shouted someone.

Onion Man flexed and posed as the pieces of mango landed on the ground around him.

"Who are you?" asked the hero.

The question angered Banana Man, who just finished announcing everybody's names. He was also slightly annoyed that Lord Mango was just killed. The loss of one of the Fruit Freaks was nothing more than an inconvenience, but bananas famously hated inconveniences. He would need to put in extra work to replace Lord Mango, and as far as he could tell there weren't any giant fruit monsters on planet Earth.

"We're the Fruit Freaks and we are going to clean you."

Onion Man glared and slowly looked between each fruit, then shook his head. "That seems weird. Let's not do that," said the hero.

"Get him," said Banana Man.

Dame Malus cracked her knuckles and swung at Onion Man. He laughed as the fist flew through the air. It was so much slower than what he was used to dealing with.

What Onion Man hadn't considered was that he was tired from a long run, and more importantly, he wasn't used to dealing with anything because he had not had a fight in three years.

While he laughed, the fist connected with his cheekbone and twisted his head around. Onion Man looked down, saw his butt, and screamed. He tried running but ran forward instead of the direction he was facing. Captain Vitis picked the hero up, turned him upside down, and stuck his head deep into the cement. To those above the ground, all they could see was Onion Man's butt and legs wiggling and they could hear a faint, panicked scream from below.

"Take him up. We're going to run some tests," said Banana Man.

Captain Vitis nodded, pulled Onion Man out of the ground, and started walking back to the basket ship. Onion Man flailed and continued to scream and cry. Captain Vitis almost lost his footing more than once from the slickness of Onion Man's tears.

"I'll join the Captain," said Banana Man. "You two stay down here and get this city sorted out."

Madame Citrus and Dame Malus bowed. When they turned, the citizens nearby scattered. The two Fruit Freaks split up and chased the terrified citizens.

Banana Man watched with a smile as he climbed the slippery ramp. Ahead, he saw the tears streaming from Onion Man's face, who tried everything he could think of to escape.

Captain Vitis roughly brought Onion Man into the ship. The tears abruptly stopped as soon as they were inside. It was all sheen metal instead. Some small bits of wires and lights were visible along the walls and ceiling, but most of it looked more like smooth sheets of metal.

"Why does this look so familiar to Mecha Lagomorph?" shouted Onion Man.

"Mecha what?" asked Vitis. His voice was high-pitched and not at all menacing.

"The Rabid Rabbit. My previous nemesis. He looked just like your wall."

Vitis looked at the wall and stopped walking.

"Your previous enemy looked like a wall?"

"Yes. Not all walls. Just this wall."

Banana Man stepped beside them and looked at the wall as well.

"That is because I gave your friend our technology, Onion Man." Banana Man turned to him and squatted down. His weird buggy eyes stared, unblinking at the hero. Banana Man's nose touched Onion Man's. "I know who you are, Hero of Delicalopolis. The Rabbit told me all about the famous Onion Man. We're here to wipe your scent from existence."

Banana Man stood up and placed a tissue against his nose. His face turned a pale shade of green.

"You okay, boss?" asked Vitis.

Banana Man nodded by wiggling his whole body back and forth. The villain waved Vitis on and waited behind to regain his composure.

Vitis, unable to smell with some of his faces, was half unaffected by the strong odor. The faces that were affected were ignored. The grape monster was like a big democracy with one voice. Whichever decision had more faces agree to it was the one Vitis picked.

Vitis walked Onion Man to a large glass tube filled with a bubbling blue liquid. The villain lifted the squirming hero and dropped him into the container. Banana Man fastened the cover, which left Onion Man suspended in the liquid.

The hero floated with his cheeks puffed full of his last breath. He pointed to his cheeks and shrugged. It was the best way he knew to ask a question.

"The bubbles in the liquid are oxygen. You will be able to breathe there," said Vitis.

Onion Man nodded. He let his breath out slowly, creating a stream of bubbles. Onion Man whole heartedly trusted Vitis and the bubbles, but Vitis was lying. It was a pretty obvious lie. First, an alien fruit monster did not know how human lungs work, and he understood even less about the vegetable humanoid hero's lungs. He was also a villain trying to defeat Onion Man. There were so many signs that the water was not breathable, but the hero noticed nothing. He took a deep breath back in and filled his lungs with liquid. But as a superhero, Onion Man was unaffected by his water-logged lungs. Most things that would kill normal humans didn't even harm the masculine hero. He did not know why. Vitis did not know why. Nobody knew why. He was just Onion Man, and that was the only explanation needed.

It wasn't comfortable. Having water in his lungs was a new kind of sensation, and he wasn't sure how to feel about it. Was he into it? He couldn't be bothered to think about the water massaging his lungs because he was much more concerned with the buttons Vitis was pushing. Each button summoned a new apparatus that poked the hero and took samples of all different kinds. There was nothing enjoyable about the whole situation. Although, he did enjoy the tickle from the needles.

They tested and twisted and bathed Onion Man for hours. The water became so cloudy and filthy that the villains had to stop their operations. Filth spun like a whirlpool. Vitis pushed buttons in an attempt to clean the tank, but nothing seemed to change. Green chunks floated through the water and bumped into the glass hard enough to crack it.

"Is the water speeding up?" asked Banana Man.

Vitis placed his gloved hand against the glass. "It appears so," he said.

The water inside continued to spin faster and faster until the top of the tank flew across the room and lodged itself in the sheen metal wall. Water poured over the sides, dumping deposits of green filth throughout the floor.

It continued rising and spinning until the tank was empty, apart from the man lying in the middle. His orange suit was torn, nearly shredded, and faded. The color looked almost white, hardly distinguishable as orange. Onion Man's hair was disheveled and unlike anything ever seen on the handsome hero. It was a mess. He was a mess.

But there was something else different. Something much bigger that made the two villainous fruits smile and grin and giggle.

Despite the filth littering the floor of the spaceship, the malodorous scent emanating from the hero was gone. It was not that the hero smelled good or even pleasant. He did not smell at all.

And that made Onion Man weep in a fit of confused tears. His eyes didn't sting for the first time in his life, but was it a good relief? He tried to stand and found himself quickly back on his face at the bottom of the tank.

"You're powerless, Onion Man," said Banana Man. "I knew the source of your power was your scent. Now Delicalopolis is ours."

Vitis grabbed two aerosol cans from the nearby shelf and sprayed both into the air. A lovely cinnamon apple smell filled the room. Onion Man heaved and tried to fight for clean air. He suffered immeasurably, both physically and emotionally. Mostly emotionally.

"Dump him," said Banana Man.

Vitis pulled a lever. Gears whirred and lights flashed. The bottom of the tank opened and Onion Man fell into the sky. He looked around as the birds and wind flew past. Why were there so many birds in one spot? That was his first thought. His second was, "I'm going to die."

This was a significant moment because Onion Man had never truly thought he would die before. The thought had previously graced his thoughts in a very sarcastic way. Or maybe brief flashes of worry, but nothing prolonged or with much sincerity.

His life flashed before his nose, and he missed the smell. It was often reminiscent of burning hair and week old diapers. Sometimes it took on different varieties like rotting food or gym shoes, keeping it fresh for himself and those of Delicalopolis.

He wondered if the citizens would miss him. He hoped so. There was a good chance the villains only ever appeared to fight him, but he still did his best to protect everyone.

How did it take him so long to fall? Onion Man looked around. He was indeed falling, not flying. Though it felt like he was moving rather slowly.

He was actually moving rather quickly. In his swollen brain, the hero moved much slower. Time even seemed to almost freeze, which gave him plenty of time to wallow in his new philosophical thoughts.

How could he survive this fall?

"Well," he thought, "how do I know I won't survive? Banana Man told me I'm powerless, but how would he know?"

The thought surprised Onion Man. He was impressed that he managed to have such a thought. Maybe a lack of smell gave him a boost to intelligence. He knew it was unlikely. Although, everything happening was new and nobody could say what was and what was not.

Would acting like an Olympic diver give him a better chance of survival? The hero had heard that hitting water from far enough up was like hitting concrete. So was hitting concrete from far enough up like hitting water?

He hoped so because diving was the only solution he had managed to think of in his suspended time. His brain calmed down and shrunk back to its normal size.

And with that, time returned to its normal speed for the hero. While plummeting quickly towards the Earth, Onion Man positioned himself in a dive, with his hands above his head and his feet pointed back.

This was it. This was the answer he was looking for. The hero dived like the athlete he was and hit concrete.

Somehow, deep in his brain, part of Onion Man thought. Synapses fired and real brain activity took place in the split second before his death.

Whatever experiment the Fruit Freaks had done took away his powers. But they even said it only took away the powers he had from his scent. Not all of his powers were from the rancid smells of his body, and he had clearly forgotten that part.

The unconscious part that remembered that fact released itself and covered the hero in flames hot enough to melt the sun. Because Onion Man did not remember he had the fire powers, he really did think he went through concrete like it was water. It quickly melted as he dove through and cooled off just as swiftly. With his brain also on fire, Onion Man sorted through his thoughts. He was still unaware of the true source of his powers, so he had no idea that he simply took a bath. There was no connection between his hygiene and his strength. But who could tell him such an obvious fact?

Eventually, he burst into the sewer far beneath Delicalopolis and crashed into the water. The flames were extinguished and he was happy to be surrounded by overwhelming odors once again.

Over the years, Onion Man had accidentally convinced himself that his heroics and his smell were linked together. Almost like each good deed he did increased the power of his odor. This was not true. Not even almost true. His powers were not produced from the smell, and the smell was also not created by using his powers. The smell Onion Man had grown so closely accustomed to was simply horrendous body odor. It was caused primarily by a lack of showering, bathing, or any other form of personal hygiene care. All Banana Man did was give Onion Man a good bath. The waters moved quick enough to scrub at the grime all over his body and fungus growing in his armpits. It was the kind of bath an angry parent might give a child who had been jumping in mud or puddles filled with rotting fish. The hero had not experienced such a bath before, as his parents were not the type that gave baths.

Down in the sewer he felt at home. It looked like his old apartment and smelled like his underside. The curved stone walls were covered in sludge and condensation, and the flowing water around his feet was green with brown chunks.

He had oatmeal once that looked similar, and smelled about the same. Some instinct deep within convinced him not to taste the sewage, despite his fond memory of the sweet, cinnamon flavor of oatmeal.

The sewer stretched into the darkness in both directions. Very little light made its way through the drains, so Onion Man was only able to see so far down the tunnel. He wished he had some incredible ability to see in the dark, but he wasn't that kind of superhero. As far as he was concerned, he wasn't any kind of superhero at all. Not a super nor a hero.

Hardly even a man. What kind of man could swim through concrete? Maybe things swapped and he could walk on water?

The thought wasn't great for a number of reasons.

1. He was standing in water at the moment, not on top of it.
2. Onion Man did run across oceans earlier in his career.
3. He didn't swim through concrete.

His eyes scanned the tunnel walls, looking for entrances or exits or anything other than sludge. There was a slight ripple in the concrete above where it had melted and rapidly cooled, but Onion Man was not perceptive enough to notice such a small detail.

"Looks like I'm walking through the sewer," he said. And he was right. He was, in fact, walking through the sewer.

Above, Banana Man paced in circles around the ship. He was uncomfortable. Something didn't feel right. His gloves were too tight and made his arms feel numb, but there was something else as well. Something deep in his mind felt tingly like a foot waking up. Vitis tried to talk, but Banana Man silenced him with one finger held before his mouth.

"I need you quiet, Vitis. I need to think. I feel as if I am missing something."

He was.

There were clearly things different about Onion Man, and it wasn't only in his name. People below, on the planet, with names like Greg, Joy, and Carl seemed to be squishy and meaty. Banana Man didn't like meaty things. Meat pies, burgers, corn on the cob. All of it was weird and juicy and not nearly sweet enough. Onion Man was different. The man reeked and despite Banana Man's fruit-powered strength, the hero felt powerful. It wasn't often Banana Man thought back on his victims he flung from his spaceship. So why now? What was it that called to him? Not even he could survive the fall from space. Onion Man was gone and it was time for Banana Man to move to the next step of his plan.

Dame Malus and Captain Citrus corralled all the citizens near the city center. They herded the scared citizens like a bear herding miniature sheep. Many were crushed beneath the cartoonishly large shoes of the monstrous apple and orange. The Fruit Freaks stomped about while announcing, "All human citizens gather in the city center."

While the announcement was beneficial for a majority of the citizens, it didn't have the reach the villains expected. Those hard of hearing, for example, had no idea what was happening. All of the deaf and hearing-challenged people sat at home going about their normal routines. They watched television, read books, and did chores. Their days were practically unchanged. The villains never forced anybody from their homes. People in Delicalopolis had grown accustomed to following loudly yelled directions from villains, so they happily left and then less happily ran for their lives. Because of this, the deaf Delicalopians were the safest people in the whole city.

The other portion of the population the Fruit Freaks missed was the animals. Their directions specifically requested human citizens to gather. The dogs, cats, birds, turtles, rats, mice, fish, monkeys, rhinos, pumas, and other animals kept as pets within the city stayed at home or went out to visit friends. These animals, who were far more than capable of understanding and mimicking human speech, were happy to have some time off. With all the parents gone, they had opportunities to gather for parties and relax.

It was a reasonable oversight for a single villain, but a complete disappointment for a group of supervillains from outer space. One would think they would be more responsible when invading a city.

Despite forgetting about the animals, there were enough people in the streets to keep Madame Citrus and Dame Malus busy. Those who didn't run fast enough were stomped like grapes.

Mixed reviews were later given about the treatment of the humans running for their lives. Some saw it as a fair punishment for not running faster than a giant fruit could walk, and others saw it as utterly horrible in every possible way. Both sides made sense.

Above, Captain Vitis and Banana Man pressed random buttons until the door opened to the ramp. They both acted as if they knew all about the ship, but the truth was that Vitis knew what 1/8 of the buttons did and Banana Man knew how to flush the toilet and use the bidet. Hygiene was his top priority.

Despite the ignorance of Banana Man, he was still a merciless villain. He barely contained his impatience as he walked down the terribly long ramp, and he found no drop of patience left when the bottom of the ramp was crowded with terrified humans. He kicked them out of the way until he reached Dame Malus.

"What's the situation?" he asked.

"You just launched about a hundred humans across the city," she said.

Banana Man sighed and looked over the sea of terrified faces. "What are you doing with them?"

"Juicing."

"Perfect." Banana Man grinned. "We need to juice the Onion last. I'll find where his remains landed." Banana Man launched another few handfuls of citizens until he reached open ground. There was nothing keeping the citizens so compacted together. Malus and Citrus stood near each other, yet the humans closed the circle tighter and tighter like a force pushed them closer together. It was a habit the Delicalopians developed after being invaded several times.

The Fruit Freaks laughed, cackled, and giggled in the evilest of ways. Their plans weren't flowing as smoothly as they originally predicted, but they were still moving along nicely.

Down in the sewer, Onion Man discovered he was lost. Despite finding a few skeletons, the "water" at his feet and the concrete walls all looked the exact same.

There were few times in his sautéed life where Onion Man would admit that he was lost. He took four consecutive left turns and paused. Everything was starting to look rather familiar. Far too familiar. Out of all the villains Onion Man fought and defeated, it seemed like his sense of direction might be the one to finally stop him. How tragic of an end it would be.

Onion Man often thought about real onions when he was stressed. He was rarely stressed, so the thoughts rarely arose. But it was still the place his mind went to when any form of stress climbed to the top of his performance anxiety and self-esteem issues. What did onions do when they grew old? He was a near-invincible superhero who had defeated the world's strongest villains, but his back also ached in the morning. He assumed it did, at least. Onions don't sleep, so he never did either.

Without his smell, was Onion Man more human than onion? Or was he more onion than superhero? Because of his upbringing on Onion Island, he never had a formal education and knew very little about biology. The educational standards on Onion Island were sadly very poor and Onion Man's only teacher was a crab that hung out for a few days every other month. What the hero didn't realize was the crab had no real education either and made most of the information up on the spot.

Because of all of these issues, Onion Man didn't know who he was, why he was, or even what he was. Onion? Man? Hero? Scent? There were too many variables and he couldn't solve for any of them.

Onion Man continued to wander in the sewer; lost, alone, and scentless. The "water" at his feet stirred and the sound of a flushing toilet echoed through the tunnels.

"What could that sound be?" he thought out loud. The sound grew into the roar of two waterfalls. The hero pivoted and looked behind him. Two separate tunnels converged on him, each carrying its own torrent.

On the left, the "water" bubbled and gurgled in a swirling shamrock-green assault. On the right, the "water" was gingerbread-brown and carried what appeared to be dumplings.

With the onslaught of delightfully colored liquids came a scent unlike anything Onion Man had experienced. Each tunnel brought about a smell so disastrously bad that Onion Man felt the need to plug his nose. The odor was stronger than he was and far more impressive than anything he or his butt had ever produced. The hero braced himself and accidentally ignited his Fried Onion powers from deep within. Bonfire-level flames engulfed his body as the mixture of liquids struck him. The intense heat boiled the liquids and released incredible amounts of methane into the tunnel. It only took moments for that methane to ignite. The sewer gases exploded and tore the cement walls apart. It was an unlucky time for Madame Citrus to step onto the road directly above Onion Man.

She was destroyed in an instant and gallons of orange juice splashed across the sewage-stained rubble. The humans in the area all froze. Nobody had any idea what happened and they were too terrified to move.

A weird mixture of scents filled the air and people were uncertain if they enjoyed it or not. The fluid mixture from the sewer spilled its smell across the city, and Madame Citrus's orange juice fought to deodorize the air. The result was fruity sewage, which was both pleasant and terrible.

Onion Man was frustrated. He pushed rubble aside and stood in the ruins of the sewer. Smoke drifted off his skin and hunger rumbled in his stomach. Everything happened too quickly for him to be sure what had happened, but he knew he certainly wasn't happy about dealing with it all. The explosion made his ears ring and the countless boulder-sized chunks of concrete that landed on his head made him feel uncomfortable.

At least he realized he was still alive. Was it the horrible smell of the sewer that saved him? Or was it his impressive muscles? There were a lot of options running through his head, and all of them were wrong.

The hero crawled out onto the street. He stopped, stretched, yawned, and rubbed his eyes. Thunderous applause filled the air and he had no idea where it came from.

"Onion Man," shouted somebody.

"It's Onion Man," shouted someone else who wasn't listening to the first person.

More and more people shouted and cheered and ignored the observations previously made. Onion Man, who was slowly understanding what was happening, really wanted to eat a full pizza. Something about the situation really stirred his hunger into a frightful wakefulness.

The hero was uncertain how to respond to the applause. Another of the Fruit Freaks was defeated, but Onion Man didn't know what happened to her. He hardly knew what happened to himself. He still felt powerless and weak. And like someone said before, "Weakness is a sign of being weak."

He had lived by those words his whole life. Nothing meant more to him than that quote. There were many times when he forgot all about the quote, but it still lingered in the corner of his mind right next to hygiene expectations and what a healthy diet consists of. They were all important in their own way, and he couldn't forget about any of them. He also couldn't remember any of them, so it was fairly difficult overall.

Onion Man waved at the citizens, scratched his stomach, and awkwardly walked away. Their applause and hoots and hollers continued behind him as he waddled. With Banana Man and the other Fruit Freaks still present, Onion Man feared no pizza joints would be open. He was correct, for once, but that didn't stop him from stopping and knocking on the door of each pizza place.

"Hello? Is anybody in there? Are you open?" he repeated at each location.

A few stragglers walking to join the herd in the city center stared as they passed the hero. He smiled at each Delicalopian he saw, though he didn't recognize any of them. That wasn't out of the ordinary, as he didn't personally know anybody.

Onion Man continued knocking and pressing his face against the windows of each pizza place. He was set on filling his rumbling tumbling tummy with a fresh slice of pizza.

Banana Man sauntered through the streets of Delicalopolis. His eyes scanned back and forth, looking for Onion Man. He was certain the hero had landed somewhere near his current location. He was even more certain the hero had landed within the city limits.

Vitis followed from a distance, staying far enough back to hide from the banana. Vitis was concerned about Onion Man, but he was unable to share that with Banana Man. The commander of the Fruit Freaks was too angry from the scent of the city that he had trouble focusing on what was happening directly before him. Banana Man overestimated his own strength and underestimated how much a good bath can change a person.

Vitis knew Onion Man still had some sort of powers, despite wiping away his horrendous smell. He was worried about Banana Man. What if the commander stumbled into a multi-layered trap set by the city's hero?

The Fruit Freaks had taken over plenty of planets. They perfumed city after city until vegetables were eliminated from the planets, yet something felt different about Delicalopolis. The deranged rabbit they found in space had spoken harshly of the Onion. Over and over, he expressed extreme distaste for the hero, yet he also seemed to aspire to be Onion Man.

Vitis feared the hero was more than what they could see. If the rabbit's stories were true, Onion Man had already defeated villains capable of destroying vegetables. If that was true, then what would a bunch of fruit do to a monster like that?

Banana Man stomped and roared, sending cracks through the asphalt road.

"Where is the Onion Man?" he shouted. His voice shattered the windows nearby. Vitis flinched and watched his commander throw a tantrum.

"Banana Man," said Vitis. "I believe Onion Man managed to survive the fall."

Banana Man pivoted on his foot and glared at Vitis.

"Impossible. Nothing can survive that fall."

Vitis's faces changed and matched Banana Man's glare. "Consider the possibility, Banana Man. I will return to the ship to protect it. Don't count on being able to juice him just yet."

Banana Man held his glare until Vitis disappeared down an alleyway towards the city center. Banana Man continued to throw his tantrum in private until he felt sufficiently relaxed. Onion Man was still nowhere to be found, even though he asked nicely. He asked nicely several times, and still nothing. The only option was that Vitis was right, and that made Banana Man even more upset. He liked to be right.

"If he continues to roam the city," said Banana Man, "I will find him and finally eliminate Onion Man."

The hero strolled down the street. He looked at the terribly tall arcade and remembered all the times he failed to win a single pinball game. Deep inside, he got upset with the memory and pushed it away. There were more important things to think about at the moment, like remembering what he was trying to do. A recount of events seemed necessary.

1. Onion Man was writing the next best selling book
2. Weird fruit monsters from space landed in Delicalopolis.

3. Onion Man arrived and accidentally diced a mango
4. The mango smelled delicious
5. Onion Man was taken into a spaceship and bathed
6. He no longer smelled and fell from space
7. He ended up in a sewer and blew it up
8. There was no pizza.

Something seemed wrong with the list, and it was undoubtedly #8. Where was the pizza and why hadn't he eaten any?

Onion Man shook his head to try to reorganize his thoughts. They bounced back and forth in his skull with each shake, until they landed in order.

Pizza was not the priority. It took him a moment to accept that reality. Pizza, for once, was not the priority. Deep in his bones, cells, and even in the fibers of his brilliant hair, sat the desire to save Delicalopolis. The Fruit Freaks were more cruel ,uglier, and smellier than both Ice Man and the Rabid Rabbit. He couldn't stand for that. His odor needed to return, so he could defeat the supervillain team.

But how?

Onion Man had asked that question far too many times in his life. He already knew how, but he simply didn't trust his own thoughts. They could be confusing, and even misleading. Pizza wasn't the answer. Banana Man was the leader. Without him, the others would return to the dark depths of space where they came from.

Was that true? Dark depths didn't seem like the home of fruit monsters. He wasn't sure, as Onion Man was the farthest thing from an astronomer or even an astrologer. Were the fruits Scorpios or Aquariums? He didn't know.

Return the fruit basket to space. That was his new goal. As far as Onion Man's brain went, a singular goal already pushed its processing power to its limits.

Return the basket, save the city. Stop Banana Man, save Delicalopolis, and get pizza. The goal is pizza.

Onion Man quickly shook out his head until the pizza fell out. Not literally because he would eat it immediately. Only figuratively, so he was once again focused on defeating the villains.

Banana Man didn't stand a chance. Onion Man jogged in place, did knee raises, push-ups, jumping jacks, and just spun around in a circle because he thought it was a workout. The sun passed through the sky, disappearing over the horizon, and climbed back around on the other side. Over and over, the sunset and awoke. Onion Man continued his rigorous, non-stop workout until drops, small driblets of sweat formed deep within his armpits.

He worked out vigorously, but the sweat that presented itself was weaker than a soggy tortilla shell. It wouldn't be enough. Onion Man thought back to the training sessions he had on Onion Island that brought him back from his failure against Ice Man. Would a pineapple fish show up once again to say the city was in need? He assumed no, as he was nowhere near a body of water.

But fish can walk? He didn't know. He swam through concrete days ago, and that didn't seem like something that was possible. If a fish appeared and asked for his help, he would readily give it. Deep in his mind, he hoped a fish wouldn't appear for another day or two so he could properly work up a sweat.

Onion Man worked out as well as he could, churning the ground below him into butter as he pounded his heels into it over and over and over again. None of his muscles grew tired and his heart rate hardly changed throughout the week. No sleep, no food, and not a single slice of pizza. But he needed to work up a sweat. Without sweat, can odors exist? Without odors, can he exist?

Onion Man exercised for another week, churning more asphalt to butter, before returning to his abandoned apartment. The building had been abandoned long ago, as the tenants couldn't bear the smell. Bears couldn't even bear the smell. Even Onion Man couldn't bear the smell.

The floor had petrified and each step hurt Onion Man's feet. Potato chip crumbs had turned into fossils and poked at the delicate soles of his feet. His whole apartment seemed like it could be added to a museum of natural history. Rare fungus grew along the walls and in the back of his television, and he swore he saw some extinct animals slither behind dressers and cabinets. Onion Man even swore he saw a Tyrannosaurus Rex, but he didn't have any proof. It hid too well within the realm of his apartment.

After a long trek to his bedroom, Onion Man sat on his bed and heard the sheet crack like a layer of ice atop a lake. He took a deep breath and massaged the bottoms of his feet. To feel like a hero once again, Onion Man needed the suit of a hero. The only place in Delicalopolis that could possibly have a superhero's suit was his own closet. So, what were the chances he would find such a suit in the decrepit place?

Onion Man took careful, planned steps around the petrified shag carpet. Each thread stood like a needle and he didn't like the discomfort on his feet. Potato chips and carpet threads provided more than enough trouble for him, despite being unable to puncture his skin. And, of course, Onion Man forgot that he could just fly or hover over the dangerous, fossilized carpet.

To him, the journey from bed to closet was comparable to an explorer searching ancient, abandoned ruins for treasure. Ruins that were covered in traps and secrets, though his room had neither traps nor secrets.

The hero reached the wooden closet door and let out a massive sigh of relief. He threw the door open and accidentally ripped it off its hinges. The door barreled through the walls, tearing apart the apartment building. Onion Man focused on the contents of the closet and once again failed to notice he was still incredibly powerful.

Inside the closet hung three suits: A tuxedo, a lime green spandex suit, and a scuba diving suit. He stared at the collection for a moment, trying to recall why he owned each of the three.

As far back as his memory went, Onion Man could not recall a single instance when he wore a tuxedo. There were certainly plenty of moments where he should have been wearing one, but he preferred to only change clothes once his were ruined from battle. His beloved citizens expected to see the spandex suit, and he felt deep down that they would be disappointed if he showed up in anything else.

The scuba suit was an entirely different story. Back on Onion Island, Onion Man always dreamed of being a scuba diver. Always, in this case, means he thought about it once and many years later purchased the suit. If one looked closely, the price tags and washing instructions were still attached to each piece of the scuba suit. It was practically brand new, despite smelling like a thousand pounds of manure and being home to countless insects.

Neither suit seemed up to the task of fighting a banana. Lime green was the answer, as always, and he hoped his powers would violently return as he slipped into the suit.

The interesting thing about spandex suits for superheroes is that they do not simply slip on, as Onion Man hoped. He tugged and wiggled, shook and wriggled, and really just stretched the suit to its limits. He pulled and pulled, trying to fit the suit over his monstrous muscles.

Onion Man was undoubtedly the greatest hero in existence, yet putting on the spandex suit felt like it fatigued his muscles and made his mind weary. He sat heavily on the bed and took deep breath after deep breath.

Captain Vitis took long, awkward steps up the ramp to the spaceship. Delicalopolis faded into the clouds as he reached the door. He was growing tired of climbing up and down, but he was unable to argue with Banana Man. The Fruit Freaks needed a commander, and Banana Man was always the clear choice. Even after Lord Mango's demise, the others would all say Banana Man was their only hope.

Vitis poked buttons as he walked, hoping one would activate something useful. A radar or scanner, some way to find the Onion Man.

The Fruit Freaks had flown far across the galaxy, yet Vitis had absolutely no idea how to work the spaceship. As the ship's captain, he felt oddly responsible for knowing how it worked. The others were just as clueless, and aware of it. The forward button and perfume button were clear enough, and he was sure he could find a vegetable zapper if necessary. But what did all the other buttons and lights do? He had so many faces and so many eyes, but he still could not count the number of buttons throughout the ship. It was unbelievable.

The Captain walked back to the tank where Onion Man was bathed against his will. It still smelled earthy and rotten. It had none of the flowery, perfumey smell that all fruits longed for.

Vitis ran the bath again and watched the waters spin and splash and slosh around in circles. It spun over and over and grew darker and dirtier with each pass. He stepped back and stared at the tank. Each set of eyes opened wide and each mouth fell agape.

The water in the tank changed from murky, muddy water to glowing, fiery red. Heat spilled out and melted the indestructible glass of the tank. The water, turned lava, poured over the controls and spread across the floor of the spaceship.

"He's not an onion," said Vitis. "He's a monster."

The lava melted through the floor and spread across the ground. The Fruit Freak ran as fast as he could through the spaceship, but the onion-scented lava followed him. Vitis ran into the wall, turned, and stared at the boiling, bubbling lava. He sighed and closed his countless eyes as he fell through the floor into the skies of Delicalopolis.

Onion Man took a final deep breath and felt the air molecules dancing in his onion-filled lungs. Physically, he felt weak. He felt like a newborn puppy, without any of the cuteness. Onion Man wasn't an expert of animals or cuteness, but he was certain that a newborn puppy would have an incredible amount of trouble trying to fight supervillains. Or even regular villains.

Mentally, Onion Man felt more like himself. The squeezing discomfort of the spandex suit was familiar and refreshing. It brought him back to his days before success. Back to his days of tears and odors. Back to his roots, before being plucked from the dirt like an onion.

There was a chance he could win. Deep down he could feel something boiling, ready for victory. Realistically, the boiling was no more than irritable bowel syndrome, but it would be months before he got that handled. A renewed urge took control and drove him forward. Onion Man squatted on his fossilized bed and pushed off with his feet. Everything in his mind felt uncertain, but he decided it was time to bring back the old effort. Even when others didn't want him to succeed, Onion Man always fought back to protect the Delicate City.

With the force of three thousand farts, Onion Man exploded off the bed and through the thirty floors above his apartment. Once in the sky above, he hovered and took in the view. Below, the apartment building finally collapsed, erasing the last living tyrannosaurus rex.

Onion Man floated without trying. Effortlessly flying like a true hero. Far off, his super vision caught a glimpse of Vitis plummeting to the ground. Villain or not, that was no way to go. Onion Man dashed forward and caught the villain in the air. Vitis's faces cycled through disbelief, joy, anger, and something in between.

"You saved me?" asked the villain.

"I always save those in need," said Onion Man.

Vitis punched the hero in the face. It felt like thirty semi-trucks colliding with his flawless face over and over. Each punch rocked his head back and made him thoroughly annoyed.

"I just saved you," said the hero.

Vitis struck him again, each of his grape faces turning to the facade of pure anger.

"You are my enemy, Onion Man. I will defeat you now and prove the Fruit Freaks are the best in the galaxy."

Onion Man looked around while being repeatedly struck in the face. They were hovering, still fifty feet above even the tallest buildings in Delicalopolis.

"Well, have fun," said Onion Man. The hero heroically dropped Captain Vitis. The bunch of grapes plummeted through the air, each face showing a different expression of anger, astonishment, thrill, concern, sleepiness, hunger, confusion, a different form of concern, and a few other forms of hunger. There were a lot of grapes in the bunch. Too many for Onion Man to look at. Vitis reached out with his gloved hands and tried to clutch the air, anything to stop him from falling.

Unfortunately for Vitis, he was unable to fly or grab onto the air molecules. The villain hit the ground, tossing fresh concord grape juice across the city center.

Onion Man watched the purple juice run over the asphalt and disappear through the sewer grates. More cheering erupted below as the compacted citizens in the city center spotted Onion Man.

The super villainous apple, Dame Malus, turned her villainous gaze to the sky. She shoved Delicalopians aside until she stood in the sticky remnants of Captain Vitis. She pointed with her cartoonishly gloved hand at Onion Man, and he swore he could see the purest of evils in her eyes.

As a career hero, Onion Man had seen plenty of evil. Ice Man and the Rick Rabet both looked quite evil during their brawls. Yet, something looked different about Dame Malus.

As a vegetable-based hero, Onion Man had very little experience with fruits. His diet consisted almost entirely of pizza and potato chips. It was disgusting to the average person, but nobody was going to tell the hero of Delicalopolis that he had a bad diet. Nobody except the dietitians, but Onion Man didn't even know they existed. Dame Malus's glare was a new form of evil to him, an apple-based hatred. After defeating three of the Fruit Freaks, he figured he had seen all there was to their fruity hatred. He was entirely wrong.

Dame Malus squatted into a battle stance and screamed. Her voice echoed down the street, shattering any remaining windows in downtown Delicalopolis. Her color changed in flashes from deep red to bright green and a weird flash of blue. The street around her exploded. Debris floated into the air and broke into smaller and smaller pieces.

"I think she is powering up," shouted some unknown citizen below.

Onion Man's super-hearing picked up the useful information, and he too decided to power up. The problem was that he had never once powered up. There was never a need before. A training montage was usually more than enough preparation for a big fight. While floating in the air, Onion Man copied Malus's stance and shouted just as loudly.

He had to fight furiously to not poop his pants as he screamed and flexed each muscle in his body. Abs wiggled, butt cheeks wriggled, and biceps twitched uncontrollably. Onion Man knew shouting and flexing wasn't going to make him more or less powerful, but he did enjoy the competition against Dame Malus. They each tried to scream louder than the other, back and forth for hours. The citizens in the city center, unaware that they could just leave, covered their ears and watched the villain and hero face off in a shouting match.

After six hours of shouting and flexing, Onion Man accidentally combusted. Flames erupted from his body and changed the sunset into a sunrise. Clouds nearby evaporated and vanished as unbearable, unbelievable heat exploded from the Fried Onion.

Dame Malus stood from her fighting stance and watched the burning Onion Man floating in the sky, like a beacon.

"What is he?" she said quietly.

"Our hero," said a Delicalopian that was standing far too close to the villain. Malus picked him up and tossed him to the side.

Onion Man bolted through the air and collided with Malus. She caught him and suplexed him into the concrete at her feet. The Fried Onion melted through, falling back into the cavernous maze of sewage below the city. Malus stood at the surface and watched as the hero boiled the sewage and ignited the methane within moments. The whole city center exploded, launching the citizens and Malus throughout Delicalopolis.

Pain ripped through Onion Man's nose. Smells of incredibly potent awfulness filled his senses. It was the worst of everything the city had to offer. The malodorous air invigorated him. His eyes darted between the citizens as the flames across his body were unconsciously extinguished. The hero dashed through the air, catching each Delicalopian. He placed each carefully down on the ground throughout the city. Meanwhile, Malus continued catapulting through the air like a medieval cow.

Banana Man strolled through the streets of Delicaopolis, unaware of the brawl between Malus and Onion Man. The villain commander took long strides and walked with a weird swagger like he thought each step was that of an unknown dance. He looked ridiculous and everybody would have told him so if anybody saw him walking about.

His wide, unblinking banana eyes scanned each crevice, each hole, each alleyway of the delicate streets. Yet, no sign of Onion Man emerged. Nothing made sense to the villain. He washed away the hero's powers and dropped him from an incredible height. He could not have possibly survived such a fall. Even a meteor couldn't survive.

Was an onion more powerful than a meteor? It was a ridiculous thought, but Banana Man couldn't spot the hero anywhere. The possibilities were feeling more and more limited as he searched each street. Banana Man even checked the dumpsters and trash cans throughout the city, and he found nothing more than pizza boxes and discarded vegetable skins. Did anybody in Declicalopolis eat fruit? Was his conquest lost on the humans?

While he wanted to eliminate the vegetable hero, Banana Man did hope he could also enlighten the population to the benefits of fruit. Bananas were great in smoothies, by themselves, and even on toast. There were endless possibilities to the uses of fruits, but the humans in the Delicalopolis just kept putting zucchini and onions on every dish. They ate chocolate chips and carrots, or pizza with olives and peppers. Where did it end with these people?

Was the perfuming from the Fruit Freaks wasted on these people? Did the Rabid Rabbit lie to them? If Delicalopolis was lost to their message, how would the rest of Earth respond? Was there more to Earth? Banana Man couldn't say for sure because all he saw during their descent was clouds. If the rest of the planet was only clouds, they would have a tough time convincing them to switch to a fruit diet. Clouds on any planet aren't known to feast often, especially not on sugary fruit.

The cloud people of Zippulon VI had no interest in food, other than condensation. Banana Man had tried to introduce them to the condensation versions of fruit juice, but they had no interest. How could the Fruit Freaks conquer planets if nobody would listen? Clouds were quickly growing to be his new least favorite type of person. Onion Man was his least favorite, but as far as he could tell, onions weren't a type of person.

He had been wrong before. And he was again. Onion Man was clearly a type of person. An onion person.

Onion Man set the last citizen safely on the ground and reignited his Fried Onion flames. The city smelled of caramelized onions because Onion Man's blood was 99.89% sugar. He sniffed and sniffled and sniffed again and noticed his scent. It was weirdly pleasant. No tears were formed, other than those from joy. He wept in a happy way, rather than his eyes burning from terrible smells or from overwhelming disappointment.

He was the Caramelized Onion and he was ready to fight. Or was it the Fried Onion? Green Onion?

Red Onion?

It didn't matter. Onion Man was a hero and he was ready to finally fight again. He was the Onioniest Man to ever exist.

Onion Man sprinted through the streets, turning the asphalt into lava. The Fried Onion ran and ran and jogged, walked for a minute, then ran again until he found Dame Malus. The apple monster was once again powering up, shifting her color from a pleasant red to a sour green, and everything in between.

"Time to caramelize you," shouted Onion Man.

Dame Malus stood from her battle stance and glared at Onion Man once again.

"What a bizarre thing to say," said Malus. "What will it take to defeat you?"

Onion Man's flames vanished. The hero stood before Dame Malus, all dumb and exposed.

"Honestly, in the past, all it took was a well-placed insult or observation that made me feel like a bad hero. Now, I'm not so sure. It might take something more intimidating or threatening than something that hurts my feelings."

"You are a bad hero and you're incredibly ugly."

Tears blurred Onion Man's vision. He turned his back to Malus and sniffled loudly. His feelings were hurt. More than hurt. They were wounded beyond repair. It felt like he needed stitches for his feelings.

Onion Man used his skin-tight sleeve to wipe away his tears, then pivoted on his foot and faced Malus once again.

"Your malice won't hurt me, Malus. I am more powerful than you could ever imagine." Onion Man flexed and ignited his biceps, just to make Dame Malus feel a little scared.

Surprisingly, the apple wasn't as scared as he hoped. She flexed in return and apple-scented perfume spread through the air. Onion Man was caught off guard, and the fruity scent of Malus's sweat made his stomach churn.

Onion Man spun again, turning his back to the villain. With deep concentration, Onion Man focused all of his powers inside his body. Internally, the Onion, Fried Onion, some other random powers, and indigestion all combined to form the most spectacular fart ever created.

Malus's perfume-like apple scent floated gently and delicately through the air until it reached the unstoppable, horrible, powerful force of Onion Man's gas. The fart ripped through the air like a thunderstorm, striking down anything not malodorous. It was as if bolts of lightning literally attacked the good smells and turned them into horrendous onion-scented farts. Even Onion Man's eyes watered in the onslaught produced by his toned onion butt.

"Are you ready?" asked Onion Man politely.

For those unaware of how battles normally happen, asking if the other is ready is both polite and honorable. In the case of Onion Man vs. Dame Malus, it was an unreasonable question. Malus had always been ready to fight vegetables, and she had mentally prepared to ignore anything Onion Man said. His kind words passed right through her ripened ears.

Malus placed her palms together, then thrust them forwards. A blast of energy ripped through the air. Sprays of chunky applesauce flowed from the beam as it struck Onion Man in the chest. The hero was launched backwards, causing him to tumble through his beloved city once again. He crashed into buildings, bounced off concrete, and managed to get three strikes while falling through the bowling alley.

He stuck the landing like an Olympic gymnast and thrust his hands in the air to impress the judges. His brain had bounced around a bit too much within his skull, so he forgot that there were no judges rating his current battle. It was good that he forgot because he would have been thoroughly disappointed if he had remembered.

Onion Man looked around the desolate part of the city he had landed in and tried to spot a glimpse of Malus. He was, of course, unaware that the section of town was only desolate because he just crashed into it. Before his arrival, the city was one of the last prospering areas. The pets, allowed to roam free, had successfully invested their money into Delicalopolis. This new pet collective was set to draw a profit within the month. A profit that would uplift the entire city from the damage caused by the Fruit Freaks.

Unfortunately for the city, Onion Man's fart-filled fall had destroyed many of the improvements the free pets had put together. A puma stealthily gathered the other representatives and started their work over in the depths of the Delicalopolis underground.

Malus arrived in a thick cloud of perfume. She was absolutely sweating juice and it smelled delicious. Onion Man let his irritable bowel syndrome loose and rocketed towards Malus on a constant stream of chunky farts.

All of Dame Malus's work to purify the smell of the city was quickly erased as Onion Man hit her in the face. The villain rolled across the ground and spun like a top until she was able to place her feet on the ground.

"You stand no chance, Onion Man." Malus brushed the dust off her skin. "You can't even beat me, and Banana Man is at least two and a half times stronger than I am."

"You underestimate me, Fruit," said Onion Man. He ignited his odor and burned brightly as the Fried Onion. "I'll make a pie out of you."

Malus's weird apple eyebrows shifted as she looked at the hero. "That's kind of messed up. I didn't say I was going to make a dish out of you."

"Well, what would you make?" Onion Man's flames dispersed as he leaned against a nearby wall and watched Malus pace and think.

"Pickled onions? Cheesy baked onions? French onion soup?"

Onion Man shook his head with each of Malus's suggestions. He didn't like the sound of any of them. The answer he was looking for was onion pizza. Literally just crust, sauce, cheese, and a ridiculous amount of onions. Like at least five entire onions. That was the only dish he was willing to be part of, whether or not he was actually an onion. Because of his invulnerability, Onion Man had rarely, if ever, been injured and had no idea what was beneath his skin. Was it layers of onions or was it squishy human flesh? Was he maybe a rotten yam and just misunderstood his whole life? There were many possibilities, all of them wrong. He was a superhero. Nothing less, and definitely nothing more.

"All of your answers are as evil as you are," declared Onion Man.

"At least I don't make people cry with my scent."

Onion Man cried. Not from her scent, or even his own. He just cried. It seemed like it had been a long time since his last weep, so he wept like a newborn. It was invigorating.

"Let's finish this," said the hero. He looked at Malus with tears welling up in his eyes and running down his cheeks. His odor was visibly rising off his shoulders as green fumes. He was in his ultimate form.

Malus gritted her apple teeth and charged. She struck Onion Man with a massive fist, but the hero didn't move. Onion Man caught her fist in his sweaty palms and pushed it aside. Malus reeled, unsure of where Onion Man's incredible strength came from.

It came from him, of course. It was unclear what she didn't understand. Where else would strength come from?

Onion Man ignited into the Fried Onion and hit her with an uppercut. Hot apple cider sprayed into the sky like a giant fountain.

The Caramelized Onion stood in the apple rain, each drip sizzling off his superheated skin.

"I'm coming for you, Banana Man," he said quietly to himself. There was literally nobody else nearby to hear him, and Banana Man certainly couldn't hear him. The villain didn't even have proper ears. Most bananas didn't have ears.

Banana Man watched the sky as storm clouds formed and apple juice rained throughout the city. It helped the unbearable heat and the horrendous smell, but it also seemed disturbing to him.

"Malus?" he thought. There was no way she could have been defeated. Who was there within the horrible city of Delicalopolis that could defeat such a powerful fruit? As Banana Man rounded the corner, he stepped in a pile of grape jelly and tried to shake it off his foot.

"Vitis? Impossible." Banana Man ran through the city, each step causing a miniature earthquake to rumble through the delicate foundations. He continued until he found bits of orange pulp scattered about the walls and street lights of the city center. Humans were spread about scratching at the orange peels.

"What do you think you are doing?" shouted Banana Man.

"Zest," said one of the citizens. The others nodded their agreement.

"Madame Citrus?" asked the villain.

The same citizen nodded. "She's delicious."

Banana Man was conflicted. He lost all of his dear friends, making him the last survivor of the supervillain team. At the same time, the humans were eating fruit more than they ever had before. The fruit was his friends, but it still counted in some weird, twisted way.

An impact ripped the ground apart behind Banana Man. He turned with his fists raised, ready to fight. Before him stood a renewed, reodored Onion Man. The smelliest hero stood from the rubble and awkwardly brushed off the dust. Onion Man thought he looked cool, but he did it all so slowly and weirdly that Banana Man felt embarrassed for him.

"Surrender or we will have to fight," said Onion Man.

"How did you survive the fall?" Banana Man sat on the ground and relaxed. He didn't feel up to fighting at the moment and just wanted to learn what happened.

"I swam through concrete." Onion Man puffed out his chest and flexed his arms.

"That..." Banana Man cleared his throat. "Great. How did you get your powers back?"

Onion Man pointed to his butt with a flexed arm. "I sweated and farted until the smell came back. You cannot defeat body odors."

Banana Man gave Onion Man a thumbs-up to express his understanding. As a giant banana, he was unable to nod or shake his head.

"I am sad from the loss of my friends, Onion Man. I do not wish to punch you or be punched by you. Is there another way we can determine who is more powerful?"

Onion Man walked up and sat beside Banana Man. He reached out and placed his hand on the villain's peel. "We could play a game. Whoever wins gets to keep Delicalopolis."

"What game?" asked Banana Man.

"Tic tac toe," said Onion Man confidently. There was no other game that could match the intensity of battle over an entire city. Tic tac toe was the only game Onion Man could think of that he could win and would be a great end to his memoirs. An end only because he never expected to fight again. He hoped he didn't lose, or the end of the memoirs would be much worse. Really a bad story ending.

Banana Man agreed. Judges from all corners of the city gathered with camera crews and reporters to cover every play.

"Best of three?" asked Banana Man. It was customary on every other planet he had visited. One wasn't enough to decide, two could equal a tie, and more than three always ended up being too much.

Onion Man violently shook his head. "Best of one. Win or lose. Nothing else to it."

The hero lit his foot on fire and drew the gameboard into the cement. He gestured for Banana Man to go first. Internally, Banana Man thought about all the ways Onion Man might be trying to deceive him. Going first was obviously the best option. It was nearly impossible to win without going first, yet he was just giving the advantage away. What was wrong with Onion Man?

Inside Onion Man's head, a dinosaur danced around to nonexistent music. He watched Banana Man place an X in the middle of the board without a single thought passing through his head. No analysis or plan existed within his brain.

Onion Man placed an O in the bottom left. The crowd went crazy and reporters and commentators talked endlessly, analyzing and predicting the next move. There was so much riding on it that the entire city felt tense, like it was holding in a powerful fart.

Banana Man placed an X in the bottom center. The crowd gasped and recoiled, anxious to see what their hero would do. Banana Man only needed one more spot to win. Would Onion Man block the villain's victory?

Onion Man blankly stared at the game bored. He stared and breathed deep. The rest of the city, even Banana Man, held their breath. What would happen?

Onion Man stretched down in slow motion. Each person gasping, crying, or screaming. The hero reached for the top center to block and the city cheered. Before playing his move, Onion Man quickly shifted his hand and placed the O in the top right corner.

The citizens of Delicalopolis wailed and wept. They lost and would forever be subject to the torture of Banana Man.

Banana Man stood and thrust both arms in the air. "I win," he declared.

Onion Man stood and looked over the board. He wasn't sure how tic tac toe was played, so he didn't understand why the villain had won. What did he do wrong? Did he do anything wrong? Was Banana Man cheating? Villains often cheated because they were villainous, and Onion Man couldn't stand for that type of villainy.

He turned and punched Banana Man. The villain's peel exploded off his body and went sailing down the street.

"I'm naked," exclaimed Banana Man. "How dare you?"

The crowd cheered. None of them cared whether or not Onion Man played fair. They only wanted their delicate city to remain delicate.

"Get him, Onion Guy," shouted a new citizen who wasn't quite sure what was happening or who anybody was.

Banana Man turned and ran as fast as he could. Onion Man jogged after him. The hero wasn't thrilled with the workout. Each step caused more sweat to bead up in his armpits and run down his sides. The drops of sweat evaporated into the air, causing the toxicity of the Delicalopolis air to grow.

Banana Man was finding his jog difficult. Every breath was labored. The air felt heavy and it tasted sour. He didn't know the air could taste sour. He turned around to see how much he outran Onion Man. Within arm's reach behind him stood the hero, grinning and on fire.

Banana Man continued running backward, terrified for his life as the Fried Onion chased him.

"Leave me alone," said Banana Man. "I won. The city is mine."

"I disagree," said Onion Man. "This city will always be mine."

Banana Man opened his mouth to speak again but stepped on his own peel as he ran backward. He clenched his teeth and bit his tongue as he flipped onto his back. The villain landed roughly on the asphalt and cried from the pain in his mouth.

"Farewell, Banana," said Onion Man. The hero kicked the fruit and launched it through the air into space.

The Delicalopians cheered and roared and cried and had all sorts of feelings. They had been so terrified.

There was actually a ton of work to do because of all the destruction and fruit juice, but they liked to pretend it was a good time to relax.

Onion Man sat down in the city center and watched as the citizens walked about, uncertain of where to go or what to do.

The mayor sat next to Onion Man and patted the hero on the back. "We're proud of you," he said.

"I haven't seen you in so long," said Onion Man. He poked the mayor's cheek. "Is it actually you? I didn't think you were around anymore."

"Oh, I'm very much around. Is there anything we can do for you as a reward for saving us again?"

Onion Man thought with all his might. What could they do? The hero heroically cleared his throat and pointed at the mayor. "I would like a new apartment and a large pizza."

"I can give you a new apartment."

Onion Man shook his hand. "Deal."

The citizens of Delicalopolis built new statues of Onion Man and repaired the streets with rubble from broken buildings. It made for ugly statues, bumpy streets, and unstable buildings.

They built his new apartment deep in the sewers, away from any living creature. It was bigger and much fancier than his old home, and he wasn't sure he liked that.

Delicalopians called it the Onion Lair. The mayor hoped it would act as a new base for the malodorous hero.

"Will you continue to protect us?" asked the mayor.

"Under one condition: You publish my memoirs."

And so it was done. *The Delicate Man* went on to become a bestseller in the very niche market of foul-smelling superhero autobiographies. It was actually the top and only of its list.

Onion Man was their hero and there was nothing they would change, except maybe the smell.

Made in the USA
Middletown, DE
08 July 2022